DISCOVERY OF DESTINY

STONECROFT SAGA 2

B.N. RUNDELL

WOLFPACK
PUBLISHING
— EST 2013 —

WOLFPACK PUBLISHING
— EST 2013 —

Discovery Of Destiny

Paperback Edition
Copyright © 2020 B.N. Rundell

Wolfpack Publishing
6032 Wheat Penny Avenue
Las Vegas, NV 89122

wolfpackpublishing.com

Paperback ISBN 978-1-64119-969-8
eBook ISBN 978-1-64119-968-1

Library of Congress Control Number: 2020931457

DISCOVERY OF DESTINY

Dedication

To my wife, Dawn. The love of my life for fifty-three and more years. She is the reason I draw my next breath. Shall I compare thee to a summer's day? Thou art more beautiful and more temperate!

1 / West

They had fought their way through Shawnee renegades, river pirates, and bounty hunters, and now stood on the slopes above the west bank of the Mississippi River, their first destination on what could become a lifelong journey into the wilderness. Their dream had long been to explore the territory beyond the civilized world and make their mark where others had never trod. Although forced upon them, this journey promised to be the fulfillment of shared visions and hopes stemming from two youths in the woods and a lifetime of reading journals, books, and more. Now they looked upon a wilderness where only moccasin prints showed the passage of man, and few others dared leave their mark.

The pink hues of the rising sun painted their backs as the two friends stood atop the lone knoll and stared at the wild lands that stretched beyond their imaginations and faded in the distance to a muted grey mist that lay like a downy blanket along the western horizon. Their stares were locked, not on what they saw, but on what they believed and the abstract images they had long shared, if only in their dreams. Before them were miles upon miles of splashes of color as the cool winds of fall painted the blushes of orange, gold, red, and innumerable of shades of auburns and browns wherever they looked. In the minds of Gabriel Stonecroft and Ezra Blackwell, it appeared the Creator had momentarily laid down his palette of colors as He sat back to enjoy His handiwork.

Gabriel's shoulders lifted as he breathed deep of the morning air, then turned to his friend, "It's almost hard to believe we're finally here. Our feet on solid ground, no one near, and the West lies before us."

Ezra grinned, glanced down at their long shadows that stretched down the hillside, then turned back to the rising sun. "I do believe God has shone His light for us to see the way we are to go!"

Gabriel chuckled, "There ya go, preachin' again!" He looked at the splashes of pink that covered the eastern sky and bounced off the waters of the Mississippi river, "But, perhaps you're right. So, for right now, how 'bout we get back to our horses and get packed? The captain said it was two, maybe three days to New Madrid, and that'll be our last chance for resupply."

"And the last chance for a home-cooked meal!" grumbled Ezra, following Gabriel down the trail to the horses.

"Home-cooked? You mean store-bought! But from what the captain said, there might not be any place you can buy a meal. He said there wasn't much there, said it's only been there for five or six years now. Before that, it was a French settlement, so maybe . . ."

"I like French food!" declared Ezra.

"You like any food you don't have to cook yourself!" declared Gabriel, pushing his way through the thick brush to the clearing. They had disembarked from the flatboat that had carried them down the Ohio River from Pittsburgh at first light, bidding good-bye to their traveling companions of the last three months.

The clearing was at the tree line that marked the beginning of the sandbank of the Mississippi River. Captain Lucius Schmidt and friends had started their trading trip in Pittsburgh, and Gabriel and Ezra had been a willing part of the crew in exchange for passage for themselves and their horses that now stood waiting in tall grass watching their approach.

Four horses, a sorrel mare and a chestnut gelding that were the packhorses, the big bay gelding of Ezra's, and the tall black stallion of Gabriel's, lifted their heads as the two familiar figures approached. The black was an Andalusian his father had traded for from a gypsy who was anxious to leave the country, that had suddenly become unhealthy for him and his family. Around Philadelphia, folks weren't too friendly to the traveling gypsies. The big black had become Gabriel's from his first day on the Stonecroft estate.

Gabriel's father was a wealthy self-made man who had built his fortune through wise investments and trades. In the process, he had also amassed a collection of weapons that spanned the history of warfare over the last two hundred years. His father had outfitted him from that collection when it became necessary for Gabriel to leave Philadelphia. His leaving was the result of a duel that came about when Gabriel found it necessary to defend his sister's honor against the son of a wealthy and disreputable man who had many powerful friends and connections in Philadelphia, both in Congress and the courts. When Jacob Wilson, the father of the slain Jason, wanted vengeance, he would stop at nothing to get his revenge. To save his family from any further embarrassment or harassment, Gabriel chose to leave, and his good friend, Ezra, would not be left behind.

As they packed their gear, Gabriel's mind wandered back to his home and his father and sister. Although he had a good life there—having completed his studies at the university, and was set to go into business with his father—his heart had never been in the city or business. He and Ezra had spent their youth in the woods, hunting, trapping, and fishing, always sharing their dreams of exploring the wild wilderness in the Great West. Now, as he thought of his family and home, he knew he would never return there. There is a way with some men that when the wilderness holds them, it captures everything about them, and they can never find themselves at home anywhere else. And with the West before them, there was no limit to what might await.

Gabriel swung the Dragoon saddle onto the back of his horse, Ebony, slipped the saddle pistols into the holsters that hung on either side of the pommel, then slid the Ferguson rifle into the long scabbard that rested beneath the fender leather on the right side of the saddle. Beneath the fender on the left side nestled the sheath containing the Mongol bow. His bedroll was tied behind the cantle, and the quiver of arrows hung on the left side, behind the rider's leg.

Although the Ferguson looked little different than Ezra's Lancaster long rifle, both being flintlock rifles, its main difference was that it was a breech-loader, and as such, Gabriel could get off between six and ten rounds per minute, compared to the two or three of the usual shooter with a flintlock. His pistols were also unique, the saddle pistols being French-made double-barreled over/unders with unique waterproof pans. His belt pistol was also double-barreled but was a turnover that required the shooter to revolve the two barrels and locks before firing the second barrel. All his weapons were rare and came from his father's extensive collection, making Gabriel exceptionally well-armed.

Gabriel's image was deceiving. A young man of nineteen years, he stood just over six feet tall and weighed a good one hundred ninety pounds. A good-looking and confident man with sandy-blond hair, moss-green eyes, a square jaw, and high cheekbones that framed chiseled features and an aquiline nose, he was lithe but powerful. He had trained in boxing under Daniel Mendoza, a three-time world champion and also with Gentleman John Jackson, an up-and-coming fighter. But it was his training in Akiyama Yōshin-ryū and that style of Jūjutsu that developed his own style of fighting and kept him in excellent physical shape. Gabriel was a soft-spoken man and was never anxious to enter into any conflict. Usually quite the opposite, as he would go out of his way to avoid any problem—especially after what had happened in Philadelphia that ended the life of a man who he had considered a friend, albeit not a close one. Jason Wilson had always been a braggart and would-be bully and relished any opportunity to exert his father's influence over those of lesser social bearing, but when he chose to deal in insults about Gabriel's sister, Gabriel had been forced to defend her and her honor.

Gabriel shook his head at the memory, lifted his eyes to the hilltop they just descended and pictured the vast panorama they enjoyed and let that image fill his mind and chase away the demons of his past. The bounty hunters who had been dispatched by old Jacob Wilson, who sought Gabriel's head in a bucket, had been killed, and it would be a long time before word would get back to the Wilson clan. By that time, he and Ezra would be long gone, although not easily forgotten.

They swung aboard and pointed the horses to the southwest, destination New Madrid, Spanish territory. "The captain said this," waving his arm to take in the country before them, "is Quapaw territory. But he said there," he pointed across the river, "is Chickasaw. He said the Quapaw are a friendly bunch, but there were also Osage, Tamaroa, and others," Gabriel shared, looking over his shoulder at Ezra. They let the horses have their heads and follow the faint game trail through the thick woods.

"You're just a bundle of encouragement, aren't you?" drawled Ezra. He was the son of the pastor of the Mother Bethel African Methodist Episcopal Church in Philadelphia and often referred to himself as Black Irish since his mother, Colleen Dubh O'Neill, said she was descended from the ancient Celts who traced their origins to the Vikings. Standing five feet eight inches and carrying a solidly built one hundred seventy pounds, he was wedge-shaped, broad-shouldered, and narrow-hipped. Gabriel said he was as strong as an ox. He had short black wavy hair and a broad flat nose that separated the deep black eyes that stared out from under his thick brow. The two men could not remember a time when they were not the best of friends, and they were always seen together. Ezra had thought it only natural that when his friend was in trouble and had to leave, they would leave together, and so they had.

After almost four hours in the saddle, the men, more used to the rolling deck of the flatboat than the ambling deck of a horse, reined in for a midday break for both men and beasts. They picketed the horses within reach of both water and graze, then put together a small fire to brew some coffee and warm up the leftovers from their last meal aboard the broadhorn. As they sat back, enjoying the coffee, Ezra asked, "You doin' alright?"

Gabriel knew what his friend asked. The recent news of his father's death, received by letter that awaited him in Cincinnati. Gabriel had grown somewhat introspective and quiet. He looked to Ezra, "Sure, sure. It was a blow, but I think he knew it was coming. The way he talked when last we spoke at home, it was like he knew, somehow. He had never said he was sick or even felt bad, but with my leaving and then Gwyneth, it was like he had no reason to go on."

"Where'd your sister go?" asked Ezra.

"She was seein' a lot of Hamilton Claiborne. You remember him, the sissy-lookin' kid who was studying for the law. According to the letter Lawyer Sutterfield wrote, she married him, and they set off for Washington. He said they're still talkin' about moving the capital there, and he wanted to be in place to make all the right connections."

"But what about your home place?"

Gabriel looked a little wistful, then forced a grin, "Father had made arrangements in his will for Gwyneth to get a good allowance, and he told me he would have the lawyer sell everything and put the money in a fund for me to draw on as needed. Then the lawyer asked if it would be all right for him to buy the place, so I'll post a letter when we get to New Madrid and settle things with him."

"So, you don't have much reason to go back to Philadelphia then, do you?" asked Ezra.

Gabriel's eyes glazed as he remembered his home and family, then looked up to his friend, "No, I suppose not. But that doesn't mean you can't."

Ezra chuckled, "Since my mum passed, Pa and I haven't seen eye to eye. And since he's been thinking about marryin' up with the Widow Baker, I think he was glad when I asked to come out here with you." He shook his head, staring at the glowing coals of the fire, "No, it seems like you and I are the only family either of us has now."

"Well, truth be told, we've always been more family than anybody else. So, brother, maybe we ought to get a move on. As much as I like the outdoors, I think I'd like to have someplace warm to spend the winter."

Both men chuckled as they gathered up their gear and saddled the horses to resume their journey. It was a beautiful day, clear blue sky, not a cloud showing anywhere, and the cool breeze of fall moved the colorful leaves like the waves of the sea, promising everything but revealing nothing.

2 / Tamaroa

Gabriel splashed hands full of water on his face, using his wet hands to wipe at his dusty neck and run his fingers through his tousled hair. He lifted himself up to his elbows, reached for another handful of water to wash the night from his mouth. Then he froze in place, seeing a strange reflection in the rippling water. A man stood behind him, watching his morning ritual. Standing just under six feet, black hair with wisps of grey hung down his back in a single braid. Tattooed on his shoulders, arms, and chest were interlocking circles and other geometric designs in umber and black. Gabriel could make out a quiver of arrows that also held an unstrung bow. The man held a long lance, beaded and decorated, with what appeared to be a scalp lock dangling near the metal spearpoint.

Gabriel slowly rose, wiped his hands on his buckskins, and looked at their visitor. He was an impressive figure with a stoic expression and piercing black eyes, and although the wisps of grey in his hair said the man was aged, his manner and stance said nothing of it. His eyes looked Gabriel over as he stood speechless then in little more than a grunt, "Why are you here?"

The words were familiar to Gabriel, having learned the basics of the Algonquian language when he studied Eliot's *Indian Bible* at the university. It was the first Bible printed in America, the first English Bible not having been printed until a hundred and twenty years later. Although he understood the Indian's question, Gabriel noted a unique inflection that spoke of French influence. He answered in English, "We have come to see this great land!" and moved his arm in a wide sweeping motion to indicate all that was around them.

"Who you are?" asked the man, also in English.

"I," responded Gabriel, putting his hand to his chest, "am Gabriel." Motioning to their camp, he continued, "My friend is Ezra. Who are you?" he asked, pointing at the visitor.

"I am Long Walker, the last of my people, the Tamaroa." The man neither moved nor changed his stance as he stared at Gabriel.

"We are about to eat. Will you join us?" asked Gabriel, miming the act of eating and gesturing toward their camp. He turned as if to go, looking back at Long Walker. When he saw the Indian move as if to follow, he continued to the camp. "Yo, Ezra, we've a visitor!" he announced.

Ezra looked up and after a double-take, said, "Come ahead on, I'm just 'bout to dig up the biscuits!" He grabbed the spade and moved aside the loose dirt and coals that sat atop the double-layered tin plates. Using his neckerchief, he carefully lifted the hot plates from the coals beneath. He sat on a grey cottonwood log and slowly lifted the top plate to reveal a circle of steaming golden-brown biscuits. "Now, that's a treat you won't often see! Grab yourself a plate and dish up the rest. There's some duck eggs an' the last of the pork belly in the pan yonder."

Long Walker followed Gabriel and mimicked his example, dishing up eggs and pork with a biscuit on the side, then sat on the end of another log and began eating. Gabriel looked to Ezra, who lifted his shoulders and eyebrows to ask the question, "Where'd he come from?" without speaking the words. Gabriel answered with a shrug, and both watched as Long Walker quickly downed the food.

"Umm, more?" he asked, looking at Ezra.

"Sure, help yourself!" answered Ezra, nibbling at his own plateful.

When finished, Gabriel and Ezra sat back to enjoy their coffee, a treat refused by Long Walker. He asked, "Where you go?"

"We're headed to New Madrid. You know it?" asked Gabriel.

"Ummm," came the simple answer, accompanied by a nod.

"Then where?" he asked.

"West, where the sun sets."

"To the mountains?" he asked.

Gabriel was surprised by his question, and he glanced

at Ezra, then back at the Indian. "Yes, we want to go to the mountains. Have you been there?"

"Ummm. Mountains have snow all time. Big," answered Long Walker, letting a slight smile tug at the corners of his mouth but not show in his eyes.

Gabriel grinned as he thought of the mountains that some referred to as the "Rocky Mountains." He was surprised that a man of the river valley could have traveled so far to the west. After considering, he asked, "You said you are the last of your people. What happened to the rest?"

The usually stoic Long Walker dropped his eyes to the ground between his feet, then looked at Gabriel, "My people, the Tamaroa, have been friendly to white men. French traded with my people and Spanish too. They brought white man's sickness," He touched himself repeatedly on his arms, chest, and face. "Sickness that marks body and kills."

Gabriel glanced at Ezra and said, "Smallpox!" to which Ezra simply nodded.

"After many died, our enemies, the Chickasaw and the Shawnee, come. They take women and little ones, kill warriors."

"How did you survive?" asked Ezra.

"I had the spotted disease of the whites." He pointed to several pockmark scars on his arms and one cheek. "I left village to die, but the Great Spirit not allow. When I come back, nothing there."

The three men continued their talk, learning more about each other. Finally, Gabriel looked to Ezra, and in that way two close friends have of communicating without spoken words, agreed. Gabriel looked at Long Walker, "Do you remember the way you traveled to get to the mountains that have snow?"

"Ummm," he answered, nodding.

"Would you come with us? To go to the mountains again? Show us the way?" asked an eager Gabriel, leaning forward in anticipation of the Indian's answer.

Long Walker looked from one to the other, then answered, "Need horse."

Gabriel smiled, "We can get you a horse. Until then, you can ride one of our packhorses," pointing to the tethered horses nearby.

"Ummm."

Gabriel and Ezra looked at one another laughing and Ezra nodded and said, "Ummm," which caused all three men to laugh together.

It was approaching mid-day when they neared New Madrid, and Long Walker reined up and dropped to the ground beside the chestnut. When Gabriel and Ezra stopped and looked at the man, he explained, "I wait far side of village."

"Don't you want to come in with us?" asked Gabriel.

"No, I wait," was his simple answer. He turned and trotted off into the woods, quickly disappearing.

"Wonder what that was all about?" asked Ezra.

"Dunno. Maybe he's had a bad experience with some of the settlers. There are those who don't like any Indians, as we've discovered," replied Gabriel. "But, let's get this done and see if we can find another horse for Long Walker."

"So, what do you know about this settlement?" asked Ezra, knowing his friend was an avid student of history and had devoted considerable study to the early settlements in Indian country.

Gabriel chuckled, "Well, if I remember correctly, this was originally a trading settlement under a couple French brothers name of Le Sieur. Then Spain took over, and Governor Gálvez appointed his impresario Colonel George Morgan to be in charge, and he recruited several American families to settle here. Only catch was, the Spanish governor required them to become citizens of Spain, and some weren't too happy 'bout that. So, no tellin' what it's like now."

"Maybe that's what happened with Long Walker. They tried to make him a citizen of Spain!" surmised Ezra, chuckling at the thought.

"Dunno, but somethin' didn't set too well with him, that's for sure," concluded Gabriel.

As they neared, they saw more than expected. A number of cabins, some of stone but most of logs, had been built in an orderly fashion, facing a road that paralleled what was obviously the main road of the village. Others were scattered nearer the trees but well-suited for defense, with shuttered windows and heavy doors. The main road held two rows of buildings facing one another, and several were of stone. Most prominently was one of a story and a half with split shingles on the roof and a carved wooden sign atop the covered porch that read, Louis Esquibel, Trader. Other buildings, obviously businesses of some sort, also had identifying signs, most in Spanish. At the near edge of town stood a large clapboard structure identified by the attached corrals and wide front door that would accommodate a drawn wagon. The two friends pointed the horses to the livery and stepped down at the door, peering into the dark interior to see a smithy banging at hot steel atop his anvil.

Gabriel waited for a pause in the metal-on-metal clang and hollered, "Hello!"

The big man at the anvil turned, showing a leather apron dirty with grease and grime doing its best to cover the girth of the typical smithy. A big grin from the rosy-cheeked man belied his size and intimidating figure as he answered, "Hello yourself! What'chu need?"

"Need our horses shod and need to buy 'nother'n. Got any for sale?" asked Gabriel, leading his big black into the dark interior.

The big man dropped the piece of hot steel into the tub of water, laid his hammer on the anvil, and removed his gloves. He stepped toward the two men, looked the horses over, and said, "I can do it. Take a couple hours or so, an' it'll cost'chu a dollar a horse!" He looked to Gabriel with a broad grin, "An' you won't find another smithy within a hunnert miles!"

"And do you have any horses for sale?"

"Got a couple out yonder in the corral. Look 'em over an' make me an offer," he replied, reaching for the reins on the big black. "I'll get started on this beauty!" He rubbed an affectionate hand over Ebony's neck and reached for the girth to drop the saddle off before he began, sparing only a glance at Gabriel and Ezra as they walked to the corral to look over the horses.

3 / New Madrid

The two friends casually walked down the main road of New Madrid, taking in the sights of the stores, businesses, and other buildings. "Look there!" declared Ezra, "That's a church! Let's take a look!" He was pointing at a large stone structure near the end of the main road, which seemed to mark the limits of the village. With a tall steeple, a bell tower, and massive carved doors, the stone structure would rival any in the towns back East. As they neared, they saw a sign in the churchyard, Immaculate Conception Catholic Church. "Boy, when those Frenchies do a job, they do it right! That's a fine-looking church building."

"It is that, but was that from the Frenchies or the Spanish?" answered Gabriel. And at the shrug from Ezra, he added, "But right now, I'd rather find a place to get something to eat. I'm surprised you haven't sniffed something out."

"Oh, I did! Right yonder, that clapboard building with the sign that says, Mamá Luna's Buena Comida."

As they seated themselves at the only available table, a broadly-smiling matronly woman with an apron over her girth came to them, "We have gazpacho and *pringá* with vegetables and *migas canas*." Although she spoke in Spanish, Gabriel understood and recognizing the dishes said, "You must be from Andalusia!" The woman's eyes flared and her smile broadened as she bowed slightly and said, *"Sí, señor ¿Y Usted?"*

Gabriel shook his head. "No, we're from the East, but not that far. And we'll have your *pringá* and more, thank you."

She bowed slightly, smiling, *"Sí, señor."* Then, leaning closer and lowering her voice, she added, "Be careful, *señor*. Those men at the corner table are evil, and they don't like men like him." She nodded at Ezra. "They will cause trouble, but please don't do anything in here."

Gabriel smiled, nodding, and said, "Don't worry, *mamá*, we won't." He watched her as she scurried back to the kitchen. Ezra leaned over and asked, "What'd she say? I couldn't hear so well."

With a slight nod toward the table of troublemakers, Gabriel whispered, "Might be in for some trouble." He had no sooner spoken than one of the men, a bearded man who equaled Gabriel's height but outweighed him by at least thirty pounds, stood and made his way to their table.

He leaned on the table, glared at Gabriel, and growled, "We don't allow folks to bring their slaves in here wit' 'em!"

Gabriel looked directly at the man, craned around to look at the other tables, then brought his gaze back to the antagonist. "Oh, but I don't see anyone with slaves here, do you?"

"What's this?" he barked, standing erect and jerking a thumb toward Ezra.

"He's not a slave." Looking at Ezra, he asked, "You're not, are you?"

"Ah, I am but a slave to my appetites and desires, and right now my appetite is raging!" answered Ezra, grinning. Then looking at the man who stood glaring at them, he asked, "How 'bout you, sir? In such a fine place as this with such great food, aren't you the least bit hungry?"

"I ain't talkin' to you!" he growled, then turned back to Gabriel, "Now, you get this negra outta here, or I'll throw the both of you out!"

Gabriel grinned at the man, then cocked the hammer of the belt pistol he held beneath the table, a sound that did not go unnoticed by the blowhard, "I suggest you return to your table and finish your meal, and we'll do the same. I promised Mamá Luna I would not get blood all over her floors, and I think it would be best if you allowed me to keep my promise, don't you?"

The big man's eyes had flared, and he stepped back when he heard the unmistakable click of the hammer being cocked. He snarled as he tried to regain his composure, "I'll deal wit'chu later!" and returned to his table. Gabriel made an exaggerated showing of retrieving his pistol from under the table and putting it back in his belt, knowing the table full of miscreants was watching.

The four men left before Gabriel and Ezra were finished

with their meal, and when Mamá Luna came to their table, Gabriel asked, "Mamá, is there another way out? It seems those gentlemen will be waiting for us and we'd rather postpone that meeting, and we need to buy some supplies before we leave your fine town."

"*Sí, sí.* You may go through the kitchen," she replied, smiling and pointing to the kitchen and the back door, "and the trader's place is right next door. You can even go in the back door. Many do all the time."

"*Gracias, mamá,*" replied Gabriel, and they quickly left the café.

As Gabriel listed the items for their order and dealt with the clerk in the trader's, Ezra watched out the window, keeping track of the band of bullies. When the order was complete and arrangements made for the goods to be delivered to the livery, Gabriel and Ezra checked the loads in their pistols and stepped through the door for their appointment. They waited in front of the trader's doorway in the shade of the overhanging porch for the lurkers to spot them, and they didn't have to wait long.

"There they are!" shouted one of the men, the smallest of the group and the usual type of hangers-on, —one who was excited by the prospect of action but seldom participated. The other three men turned, and the big man who had been their spokesman hollered, "Hold it right there!" with an uplifted hand as he started stomping toward them.

Gabriel and Ezra casually stepped from the porch into the

roadway, standing shoulder to shoulder as they waited for the others to approach. When they were within about ten feet, both men pulled their pistols and brought them level with the midriff of the menace. The adversaries stopped, starting to reach for whatever weapons they had but were stopped by Gabriel, "Don't!"

The six men stood opposite one another, until the big man said, "They can't get us all!"

Before they could move, Gabriel stopped them again, "Yes, we can! If you'll look closer at these pistols, you'll see that each one has two barrels and two locks. That means we have a bullet for each of you!" He paused to let the impact of his words sink in to the menacing band. "But here's what we'll do. I'll let Ezra here hold my pistol while you," pointing at the leader of the group, "and I settle things."

The big man growled, "Suits me! And I'm gonna enjoy tearin' yore meathouse down!" He pushed up his sleeves, revealing his muscled forearms.

Gabriel grinned and handed his pistol to Ezra, then doffed his jacket, dropping it to the ground, and with hands wide, sidestepped away from his friend, always watching the big man. Suddenly the beast roared and charged, arms held low but wide, expecting to wrap his arms around Gabriel and break bones with a bear hug. He was surprised when Gabriel stepped slightly to his left and threw the big man over his hip to fall hard on his face in the dirt. Gabriel moved back, waiting for the bruiser to get up, and was amazed at how agile he was as he jumped to his feet and charged again.

Gabriel stood firm, and as the man neared, he grabbed his collar, fell backward, and let the beast's weight carry him forward as Gabriel put his moccasins on his groin and toss him over his head to once again land on his face. This time he wasn't so quick in getting up, and Gabriel stood grinning, "My, my, how clumsy you are! You keep falling down!"

It was the manner of men in those times to face off and stand toe to toe, pummeling one another until one was knocked out or otherwise rendered unable to continue. But the training Gabriel had been given when he was in England put him always on the move and allowed him to effectively use the opponent's weight, size, and inexperience against him. Now, the big man slowly approached, holding his hands before him, and Gabriel rightly judged he was ready to try fisticuffs. Gabriel lifted his hands defensively and balanced on the balls of his feet, watching his opponent. As the big man cocked his arm for a roundhouse blow, Gabriel ducked under it and buried his fist deep in the beast's rather flaccid belly, knocking the wind out of him. He followed with a chopping blow to the back of the man's neck, knocking him into the dirt again.

Gabriel stepped back and let the bully come erect, and this time the man didn't hesitate but charged, catching Gabriel and bearing him into the dirt. Straddling him, the man snarled, "Now I'm gonna smash that purty face of your'n!" He leaned back and cocked his meaty arm to smash Gabriel, but that shift of weight gave Gabriel just enough leeway, that he arched his back, then brought up a leg to catch the big man on the side of the head and knock him off. Gabriel quickly squirmed free and stepped back, trying to catch his breath. Again, the man charged and surprised Gabriel with a quick jab that only allowed him to move his head and take the glancing blow, which was enough to knock him backwards and dim his lights for just a moment. As he stumbled backward, the man continued his charge, but Gabriel, backpedaling and trying to gain his balance, fell in front of him, making the beast trip and fall.

Both men were now on the ground, and Gabriel twisted around before the big man could catch hold. Gabriel brought up a knee to the man's ribs, eliciting a shout of pain. Gabriel knew he had broken a rib, and he jumped to his feet and allowed the man to get up again. The beast was more careful as he approached but was surprised when Gabriel ducked under his right cross and let loose with two quick right jabs to smash the big man's nose and open a cut over his left eye. The blood coursed into the man's eye and down his cheek.

Throughout the fight, the other three men had been hollering encouragement to their leader, often shouting, "Get him, Frank! Kill 'im like you said you would!" But now, after he had suffered several falls and was obviously hurt, they had fallen silent. But the big man wasn't finished. He wiped the blood from his eye and, balling his fists and flexing his fingers, snarled with a busted lip curling over bloody teeth and waded in but was met with a flurry of blows from the trained fighter, who danced around him, striking, retreating, striking, and striking again. The big man's eyes were swelling, his cheek was bleeding, and his nose was flattened and bleeding, but still he came.

As he approached, Gabriel unexpectedly dropped his hands to his side and waited. The big man didn't hesitate. He thought for sure he had the advantage, but his long-reaching jab gave Gabriel the advantage as he twisted away from the blow, grabbed at the man's wrist, and brought the big arm down as he brought up his knee, breaking the man's arm just below the elbow. The big man screamed and went to his knees, grabbing his broken arm and glaring with both hatred and fear at Gabriel.

Gabriel walked past Ezra, picked up his jacket, threw it over his shoulder, and accepted his pistol from his friend. He looked at the other three, "You might want to get him to a doctor or somebody who can set that arm. And next time? Well, if you're smart, there won't be a next time." Ezra and Gabriel walked around the others and started toward the livery as the hangers-on went to the side of their once-fearless leader.

Ezra said, "Now we know why Long Walker didn't like this town."

"Ummm," answered Gabriel, eliciting a laugh from his friend.

4 / Warnings

"He's not a good man to have as a friend, but he's even worse as an enemy!" declared the old man. He sat on a stool often used by the smithy, but more often used by his frequent visitor and longest resident of New Madrid. He leaned on his walking stick and watched the smithy finish the shoeing of the last horse and continued, "He said his name was François Ducharme, goes by Frank. But he doesn't know I knew the Ducharme family when I was tradin' up to Michilimackinac, an' he ain't one of 'em."

"So, he's pushin' himself off as somebody he ain't?" asked Ezra.

"Tain't unusual. Lotsa folks take on different names for lotsa reasons. But to take another man's name an' try to say you is who you ain't, well, that's 'nother story," surmised the old man.

"What's so special about that name?" asked Gabriel, watching the smithy trim up the last hoof of the new horse, a strawberry roan mare.

"Well, they was all traders, what you'd call *coureurs ,e bois.* You know, those fellas that go into the interior of the wild country and trade with the Indians. They never licensed up with the French to be state-sponsored voyageurs, but they's well known in the north country. Good people, all of 'em. I think ol' Frank there fancied himself to be like them. He's done a little tradin' with some, but I heard he had a bad time with some o' the Osage and Kiowa. Ain't been out in long time. Been hangin' 'round town and makin' trouble."

"So, how do they make a living? Are they farming, trapping, or . . ." queried Gabriel.

The old man chuckled and glanced at the smithy who was watching and listening as he cleaned up the leavings after the shoeing, then explained, "Lots o' folks have ideas 'bout them. There's been talk about river pirates, and most folks know them fellas traded whiskey and guns to the Indians, 'til they got run off, that is, but they don't have regular work like some folks. They been stayin' in a cabin up in the trees yonder, since the folks that was there got took by consumption."

"Well, that big fella won't be doin' much for a while," added Ezra, chuckling.

"Don't count on it. Those four been known to have others join up with 'em at times, an' they can't be lettin' folks think they can be beat. If'n I was you fellas, I'd not let no grass grow un'er my feet, nor let the sun set on my camp, if'n you know what I mean." The old man took a long draw on his corncob pipe, knocked the dottle from the bowl, and put the pipe in his pocket. "You best keep an eye on your backtrail and sleep with one eye open!" The old man used his walking stick to stand and tottered away.

The smithy chuckled, "That old man has been over the river and through the woods a time or two, and when he offers advice, you'd do well to take heed." He handed the lead rope of the roan to Ezra and turned to Gabriel, "That'll be five dollars for the shoein' and as we agreed on the horse. Now, if you be needin' a saddle, I got one I can let'chu have for a price."

Gabriel grinned, slipped his coin pouch from his belt, and dropped two Liberty Cap small-eagle ten-dollar gold pieces and a five-dollar coin into the smithy's meaty palm and watched the big man's face split in a broad smile. "Those are plumb purty! An' shiny too." He hefted them for the weight of gold and grinned again. "And I be thankin' you gentlemen, yessir!"

Long Walker stood in the shade of a colorful ash tree, the yellow and purple leaves drawing one's eyes from the stoic figure by the tall, straight trunk. He stepped from the brush as Gabriel and Ezra came near, standing as straight as his lance beside him. Gabriel greeted the man, "Ho, Long Walker!" He turned in his saddle and waved his arm toward the three horses trailing behind them, "We've got a horse just for you!"

Walker gazed at the animals. Two were loaded heavily with panniers and packs, but the third, the strawberry roan mare, was unencumbered. He walked to the speckled horse, giving her a critical eye as he held his hand toward her nose, waiting for the animal to become accustomed to his smell. He ran his hand along her neck, felt her chest, and lifted a forehoof, then walked alongside, keeping a hand on the horse's back, and stepped behind her to look at the muscular rump. He slowly nodded. "She is good horse, strong, sturdy. She will go far."

"Glad you approve. We thought we'd travel through the night, it'll be a full moon tonight, and it'll give us a good lead on anybody who might want to follow."

"You have trouble?" asked Long Walker.

"You might say that. Some fella name o' Frank Ducharme and his friends were the welcoming committee, and they didn't make us very welcome," explained Gabriel.

Long Walker scowled, and Ezra explained, "We had a little run-in, Gabriel and that Frank fella got into a little scuffle, and the big man lost."

Long Walker nodded and swung aboard the roan. "You follow," he told them, and without waiting for an answer, he trotted into the trees. They followed a dim game trail that was nothing more than a slight dip, marked only by the hoof prints of the roan.

Gabriel guessed it to be close to midnight before Long Walker, astride the roan, motioned them to a slight knoll in the midst of a long grassy flat. The night was clear, with the sky bedecked with stars and the Milky Way arching overhead. It had been cool, but now the air had a chill that reached under their buckskins and warned of colder weather.

Gabriel noticed much of the sky was dark, with heavy cloud cover obscuring the usually brilliant stars. The big moon hid behind a cloud that showed only a silver lining to betray the presence of the night's big lantern.

The men stepped down and loosened the girths on the saddles, picketing the animals within reach of ample graze. Ezra said, "I'll see if I can find some wood for a fire, and we can have us some coffee. Maybe it'll warm us up a bit."

"No fire," said Long Walker, "Chickasaw near."

"I thought they were friendly?" asked Gabriel, frowning as he looked at Long Walker.

"This is Quapaw country. Quapaw friendly. Chickasaw raid Quapaw. Saw party of Chickasaw, painted for war. This many." He held up both hands, all fingers extended. "Maybe more. Good we travel at night. Snow comes soon, cover tracks."

"Snow? When?" asked Gabriel.

Walker looked at the sky, then to Gabriel, "Morning."

They sat on the east bank of the St. Francis River, the pale grey of morning's first light at their backs. Snow had come but fell lightly and quickly melted into the warm ground. The river's gravelly bottom was visible through the clear water, and the current showed little danger. With just a glance toward the others, Long Walker pushed his roan into the water and started across, prompting Gabriel and Ezra, leading the packhorses, to follow close behind. More snow showed on their shoulders and in the manes of the horses than on the ground, but the flakes were getting bigger, and the way before them was obscured by heavier snow. Once on the other the bank, the men stepped down to give their horses a chance to shake off the excess water, although none were anxious to try to roll in the thin layer of snow.

"Black River, good trees and cover to make camp. Sun there," said Long Walker as he pointed to the eastern sky, indicating about mid-morning, "we camp."

"Sounds good, Long Walker. We'll have time to make some shelters and a good camp. What about the Chickasaw?"

"Their land beyond big river, will not go far. Stay in cover till after snow, then leave."

"Sounds reasonable. Then let's get movin', I'm hungry and wantin' some coffee!"

The wide vistas of buffalo grass and scattered shrubs soon pushed into the tree line, and the promise of shelter and warm food gave both men and horses a quicker step. The first trees hid the willow and dogwood swale, but the banks of the old river course offered additional protection as they reined up near a pair of massive fallen oaks. Between and beneath the big trunks, now devoid of any bark and sheltering a smattering of button brush and dogwood, a wide grassy bed beckoned the men.

"This is a perfect camp!" declared Ezra, "All we gotta do is cut some more brush to fill in along the sides there and over the top, and we'll have us a cozy shelter!"

"Then let's set to and get it done!" declared Gabriel. "I'll take care of the horses and you two can start on the shelter."

As Ezra and Long Walker constructed the shelter for their camp, Gabriel rubbed down the horses, picketed them, and set to work making a lean-to for their animals on the side of the big logs. In short order, their shelters were in place and a fire was going, with the coffee pot dancing and the smell of fresh coffee filled their new quarters. Three nice sized bass, impaled on sticks of willow, hung over the fire, the skins and scales browning. In a pan nearer the flames, onions, mustard greens, and mushrooms sizzled in pork-belly grease. To the side lay several pawpaws for dessert.

After the meal, Gabriel made another round of the camp, checking on the horses and the perimeter. The highest point of a knoll just behind their camp offered little in the way of a view, but the flats were more obscured by the rapidly increasing snow than by distance. The men turned in to spend the afternoon and night in their blankets, waiting for the storm to pass and wipe any sign of their passing from the trails. Tomorrow would be soon enough to resume their journey.

5 / Followed

Elbows on knees and cradling a steaming cup of coffee in his hands, Gabriel stared pensively into the flames of the early morning fire. The wee hours saw the temperatures warming, so much so that all the snow from the previous day's storm had melted away, leaving a clear sky and the promise of warm weather. The Indian and his strawberry roan were gone, having left quietly in the night. Gabriel noted that his tracks appeared to be retracing their trail of the day before and perhaps he was simply checking their backtrail, but his absence would not delay their departure.

Ezra stepped from the shelter, stood tall and stretched, yawning wide and rubbing his eyes. He looked around, "Where's Long Walker?"

"Gone," answered Gabriel, sipping his steaming coffee.

"That's it? Gone?"

"His tracks seemed to be following our backtrail, but I didn't go too far. He could be checking to see if we're being followed, or . . ." answered Gabriel with a shrug.

"Hope he likes the horse we got him. Course, we'll probably never know now," observed Ezra, pouring himself some coffee. As he sat down, he asked, "Little late gettin' 'round, aren't we?"

"Been thinkin'," began Gabriel, picking up a stick to start drawing in the dirt at his feet. "This here's the Mississippi," he drew a squiggly line from the top to the bottom of his dirt canvas, "and here's the Missouri, and here's the Arkansas." He drew the two lines to indicate the major tributaries of the Mississippi that originated west of the bigger river, one toward the north and the other further south. "Now, here's a tributary of the Missouri, the Osage River. And down here," pointing at what would be the headwaters of the smaller river, "is about where Chouteau built his trading post, Fort Carondelet. He has the exclusive rights to trade with the Osage for about five or six years, and I'm thinkin' we should head there. Maybe we'll find somebody who's been to the mountains so we can get some solid information and decide exactly where we want to go."

Ezra looked at the dirt map, lifted his eyes to his friend, and with uplifted eyebrows, wide eyes, and a grin on his face, "Good an idea as any, so sure, let's do it!" He frowned. "But what about Long Walker? Do we wait for him?"

"If we knew for sure he was coming back, yeah. But we don't know that, so, I figger we can move out and if he can't find us, he's not the savvy scout I think he is, ya reckon?"

Ezra nodded and stood to start packing up.

With the grasslands behind them, the hills were arrayed in all the colors of fall. The many hardwoods showing the reds, gold, orange, and yellow, while other species had a variety of colors from lime green to purple, a palette of colors that continued to amaze the two friends as they worked their way through. After crossing what they thought was the Current River, they sought a campsite on the south side of a long ridge that rose a couple hundred feet above the river bottom. Extending from a taller hill that stood almost five hundred feet higher, the long finger ridge lay on a foundation of stone cliffs only slightly obscured by brush and vines. Along what appeared to be a dry creek bed, a dogleg bend and deep shadow beckoned to the curious travelers. Gabriel, having dropped to the ground to investigate, pushed back some hackberries, chinquapin oaks, and sweet-smelling sumac to reveal a cliff face of limestone and dolomite. A thicker cluster of brush and vines that held a thicket of trumpet vines showed dark, and as he reached to push them aside, he saw the opening of a cave.

He turned back to Ezra, "Looks big enough for us and the horses, but I'll make us a torch, and we'll explore it a little."

"Uh, I'll let you explore. I'll stay out here with the horses," suggested Ezra somewhat timidly. Gabriel looked at his friend, "Still don't like close places, huh?"

"Nope. If I can't see an in and an out and lots of light once I'm in, it plumb gives me the creeps!"

Gabriel fashioned a torch from some big resin-coated

pinecones and some green willow branches. Once it was aflame, he stepped into the mouth of the cave, which opened up into a sizable cavern. Stalactites and stalagmites abounded in bulbous and pointed shapes, showing layers upon layers of mineral buildup. A small spring-fed stream trickled through the bottom, dropping under a ledge and disappearing into a deeper gorge, revealed only by the sound of cascading water. Where the stream followed the lower side and wall of the cavern, the floor sloped up and showed signs of cookfires of others who used the cave maybe decades or eons ago. He lifted his torch to examine the limestone wall and was surprised to see ancient petroglyphs with stick figures with lances, animals that were probably bison and elk or deer, crude drawings of bark lodges, and horses, along with geometric designs that Gabriel guessed to be emblems for lightning, storm clouds, rivers, and more. As he walked toward the back of the cavern, a different figure caught his eye, and he leaned close to see an image that was unmistakably that of a long-tusked, big-eared, mastodon. He shook his head in wonder, then, seeing the smoke from his torch move deeper into the cavern, he followed the draft into another branch of the big hollow. After a couple of twists and turns, he saw a shaft of light that promised another opening. With a little effort pushing through the brush and vines, he soon exited to find himself standing on a narrow ledge about twenty feet above the creek bottom. The ledge bent around the shoulder of the cliff face, and dropped to the bottom of the draw. Although narrow, it would be negotiable by the horses. He walked down the draw to come up behind Ezra and was pleased to see Long Walker turn to watch him approach.

Long Walker greeted Gabriel with, "We are followed."

"Oh? Who and where?"

"Six white men, a day, maybe more, behind us. They have no packhorses, and leader has bad arm, bandaged, bound." He demonstrated with his own arm held close to his chest.

Gabriel looked at Ezra, "Frank and his friends from New Madrid."

"Ummhmm."

"Let's gather some firewood and make our camp in the cavern there. Lots of good water and dry ground, and we'll be out of sight of anyone following."

"I don't wanna get trapped in no cave!" declared Ezra.

"There's a back door, so you won't get trapped. How do you think I got out without you seeing me?"

"Huh? Oh, right. Guess you did at that!"

Gabriel dragged the packs, panniers, and saddles into the cave while Ezra tended the horses, rubbing them down and letting them graze and water well below the cave on the banks of the Current River. When Ezra returned with the horses, Gabriel had the fire going and coffee on, readying the pans for the rest of the meal. Long Walker had gone hunting along the river, hoping to find a deer or elk coming down for water.

When he came into the cavern, he had a hindquarter of an elk over his shoulder. He dropped it by the fire. "Quapaw camp near, old man, old women, little ones. Gave meat."

Gabriel glanced at Ezra and back at Long Walker, "What else?"

"Their village attacked. Warriors killed, women and older children taken by Osage."

"Osage? I thought they were friendly?" asked Gabriel.

Long Walker chuckled, "Osage friendly when need to be, but they always fight and take captives and more. They are to be feared. Big." He motioned with his hand to indicate the height of the Osage, holding his hand well above his head.

Gabriel knew the Osage were a sizable people, with most of the adult males over six feet, some even reaching seven feet. They were known as an attractive people too, well-built and attired. They shaved much of their head, leaving what some would call a roach or scalp lock at the back and a single braid hanging down their back. They were also known for cutting their ear lobes for big rings or other decorations that made the lobes hang almost to their shoulders. All this passed through Gabriel's mind as he considered what Long Walker had reported.

"Do they want help?" he asked, looking to Long Walker.

"Quapaw proud people, would not ask. They have no one to help, and with no lodges or warriors, winter will take all." He looked around at the vast cavern and said, "This," indicating the cavern, "would make good winter lodge for them."

Gabriel agreed, then asked, "Could we get the captives back from the Osage?"

Long Walker frowned at Gabriel. "Maybe."

Ezra stared at his friend, "Are you crazy? Three of us going after a whole war party of giants? Why?"

"He said 'maybe.' That doesn't mean we'll do it. Let's have our supper, think about it, maybe go talk to the Quapaw, and then decide."

Ezra shook his head, "I don't know how you do it. Here we are in the middle of nowhere, a bunch of freebooters on our tail, and if that ain't enough trouble, you go lookin' for more! Why do I stick with you? Huh? Tell me, why?" He sat on the ground, shoulders lifted and hands out palms up, shaking his head.

"You like the excitement, and since we're friends, we do everything together!" answered Gabriel, grinning.

6 / Bounty

"Well, I'll be a monkey's uncle if it ain't Frank, the would-be Frenchman!" declared a slovenly man leaning against the plank counter in the only tavern on the main street of New Madrid. He laughed as he lifted his mug, "To Frank, the best swimmer in the Mississippi!"

Several of the patrons in the inn laughed and lifted their mugs with a hearty "Ho!" as they quaffed the contents. Much of it spilled from their lips and onto their chests, unnoticed as the spillage joined the other stains on their fronts. Late afternoon was just the beginning of the revelry in the tavern. The real crowd had yet to gather, so any excuse for drinking was gladly heralded and joined.

Frank and his followers paused just inside the doorway when they were greeted by the drinker at the counter, but recognition propelled them forward as they reached for mugs that were sat on the plank for them. "Frenchy! I thought you'd be dead by now!" declared Frank as he grabbed up a mug. He took a place beside the man, who had a spotted bandana tied around his head in the style of a gypsy or pirate. His loose-fitting shirt was open at the front, revealing a thick patch of black hair that blended with the long, black full beard. His eyes were full of both evil and mischief, but his smile didn't reach past his slightly parted lips. The butt of a flintlock pistol showed at his sash, as did the hilt of a scabbarded knife.

"Aw, you know us river pirates! Takes a lot o' killin' to do us in!" He looked at the bandaged arm in the sling and then at Frank's face. "What happened to you?"

"Had a accident!" growled the big man, downing the contents of the mug and banging it on the plank for a refill.

"Accident? Hah, more like a man by the name of Gabriel!" declared Squirrel, the small snake-like sidekick standing beside the larger Frank. He quickly stepped away and ducked before Frank's big arm could catch him with a roundhouse swing.

The first man suddenly frowned, lowered his voice, "Did he say 'Gabriel?'"

"Yeah! Young pup. Big 'nuff, but caught me by surprise 'fore I could defend myself!" growled Frank, slurping more of his ale.

"Was he travelin' with a negra?" asked Frenchy, scowling and leaning toward Frank conspiratorially.

Frank scowled back and answered, "Yeah, why?" Frenchy looked around the room, then pointed at the table in the corner, "Let's talk."

Once seated, the men leaned forward, elbows on the table, and Frenchy began, "We," nodding toward his partner, a greasy-looking type with stringy black hair, splotchy whiskers, eyes that never stopped moving, and a broad-striped pullover shirt atop corded britches, "were on the keelboat of Jacob Langdon. You remember him?" At a nod from Frank, he continued, "We found out about a Gabriel Stonecroft and his slave friend that had a bounty on 'em. Seems Stonecroft got in a duel and killed somebody important, and now there's a bounty on him."

"How much?" asked Frank, interested.

"At first, they said five hundred dollars, but I heard the new fella talkin' to the captain about it, and there's an additional thousand dollars if the old man gets Stonecroft's head in a bucket!"

"Fifteen hunnert dollars! That's a tidy sum, sure 'nuff," drooled Frank.

"An' the way that fella talked, the old man is stinkin' rich and might even give more!"

"But how do we collect? You know this old man who's offerin' the reward?" quizzed Frank, already calculating the shares and more.

"Shouldn't be hard. He's in Philadelphia, and a little askin' around should tell us real easy who's offerin' that kinda money."

"Hummm, yeah, s'pose so. You got friends in Philly?"

"I know some fellas that would certainly know about any reward money," answered Frenchy, grinning.

"An' they had some nice horses, an' just bought a bunch

of supplies and trade goods, and the smithy said they paid him in shiny new gold coins! We could take it all, trade with some Indians for pelts an' such, and who knows what all we could get?" declared Frank, grinning and leaning back to finish off his drink. The others laughed, and Squirrel leaned in toward Frank, "An' since Bucky's already on their trail, we shouldn't have any trouble findin' 'em!"

"You mean, you've already got somebody trailin' 'em?" asked Frenchy hopefully.

"Ummhmm. The best tracker this side o' the Mississippi! You remember Bucky Ledbetter, don'tchu?"

Nodding his head and letting a broad grin split his face, Frenchy leaned back and motioned to the innkeeper to bring more drinks.

They rode through the night and met up with Bucky Ledbetter about mid-morning of the second day.

"Another man joined up with 'em. Indian, I reckon, but he's ridin' one of their horses. They're headin' northwest. I'm thinkin' maybe they're goin' to Fort Carondelet, that new tradin' post put in by Chouteau. Don't seem to be in no hurry, neither," reported Bucky as he sat his horse beside the trail, talking with Ducharme.

"They know you're followin'?" asked Frank.

"Ain't nobody knows when Bucky's followin' 'em, you know that!" declared the tracker, showing his disgust at the insult.

"Yeah, yeah, so you say," answered Frank, then turned to

Frenchy, "We'll push on through the rest of the day," he lifted his eyes to the cloudy sky, "it's lookin' like it might storm, so we'll stop soon enough to make shelter 'fore it hits, then we'll make better time tomorrow."

Frenchy, nodding agreement, suggested, "How 'bout Bucky there goin' on ahead, make sure we don't lose 'em in the storm?"

"Good idea," answered Frank, "Bucky, you heard the man. Keep close 'nuff so they don't lose you but not too close. If you have to do sumpin' to slow 'em down, all right, but don't spook 'em!"

"Gotcha!" answered Bucky, reining his mount around and leaving at a canter. He looked at the sky and judged the clouds to be ready to drop the snow come late afternoon. He wanted to find himself some good shelter to wait it out, regardless of what Frank or anyone else thought. The tracks of the five horses were easy to follow, and he kept at a canter for most of half an hour. With his big bay gelding starting to lather up, he slowed his pace and moved to a parallel path in the thicker trees.

The next afternoon, after the clouds proved to have no more than a trace of snow, Bucky spotted the Indian checking his backtrail. He stepped down from his mount and stood beside the horse's head, stroking his neck and talking softly into his ear. With one hand on his muzzle to keep him quiet, Bucky held the lead tightly, holding the horse quiet and still. He watched as the Indian picked his way through the trees, continually searching for any followers. Bucky knew his tracks would not be found since he was wily enough to stay away from trails and to never follow the tracks of his quarry. By staying well to the side of any trail, he could more easily camouflage his own sign and go unnoticed.

As the Indian passed, Bucky looked around for his needed shelter and spotted a downed tree with ample space underneath that would be a good place for both him and his horse. They would have a warm and unobserved camp during what could possibly be another snowy night. Frank and the others were intent on getting a bounty, but he also knew Frank as one that would try to keep most of it himself. If Bucky saw an opportunity to beat them all to the payday, he would not hesitate to better his lot in life.

7 / Smoke

The bullet whined as it ricocheted off the cavern wall, once, twice, before it was lost in the darkness. A low cloud of smoke slowly filled the cave as it boiled in from the brushy entrance. Bucky Ledbetter had tracked Gabriel and company to the cave. Although they tried to cover their sign nearer the entrance, the full moon and direct path combined to paint a shadowy arrow in the rich loamy soil in the creek bottom below the limestone cliff that held the entrance.

He gathered what little dry brush he could find under the tangled thickets of button brush and dogwood nearby, stacking it near the entrance and setting it afire. As it started to flame up, he tossed some greenery atop to make more smoke and, fanning it with his blanket, he grinned as the thick grey cloud moved into the cave as if it were the smokestack of a fireplace. Although crafty and wise regarding the ways of the wilderness and tracking, he gave little thought to the movement of the smoke, that only moves with the flow of air. The only reason smoke would go into the mouth of a cave would be to pass as though through a flue to exhaust elsewhere. He just grinned, thinking he was smoking the men out of the cave, where he could kill them as they came into the open.

He moved back behind cover across the dry gulch, a stack of rocks and old logs deposited long ago by the force of a flash flood cascading down the creek after a raging storm. He hunkered down, laid the stock of his long rifle on the rotted log, sighting it on the black maw of the cavern, and waited. The smoke seemed to be thinning, and he thought he saw movement. His eagerness for the bounty caused him to fire, sending the .54 caliber ball careening into the limestone cave and ricocheting off the walls. But there was no other movement, no shouts, no rifle fire. He chuckled. *Mebbe that smoke done 'em in an' all I'll hafta do is pick up their bodies!*

The first hint of smoke brought Gabriel instantly awake. Their cookfire had long been out, and nothing but the damp air of the cavern should he be breathing. The nervous pacing of the tethered horses brought him from his blankets as he nudged Ezra with his foot to receive a whispered, "I'm awake!"

"I'll light us a couple torches from these pinecones. You load up the packhorses!" ordered Gabriel.

"Where's Long Walker?" asked Ezra, quickly pulling on the latigos of the packsaddles.

"He left in the middle of the night. Said he didn't like stay-

in' in the cave, wanted to see the stars or somethin', I dunno,
but he left."

The torches flared, causing the horses to shy back a couple of steps, but when reassured by the familiar voices of the
men, they settled down and followed as Gabriel led them all
toward the back entry. Just before reaching the opening, they
heard shouting from the cavern, but the words were garbled.
As Gabriel stepped into the clear air of early morning, the
grey light showed the shadowy but narrow trail down the
face of the cliff. He spoke a warning to Ezra, "I'll take Ebony
down and come back up for the packhorses. This shelf trail is
too narrow to try more'n one at a time."

Within a few moments, all the horses were at the foot of
the cliff, and Gabriel suggested, "Let's picket 'em here, then
we'll split up and see who's doin' the shootin'!"

The rear opening sat above the creek bottom of a smaller
runoff creek that fed the larger one at the front entrance.
Gabriel cut across the small gulch and into the trees on the
far side, leaving Ezra to stay on the face of the ridge above
the main cave. Each man stealthily picked his way through
the trees and undergrowth, aided only by the dim light of
early morning. Nothing stirred. The usual scolding chatter
of squirrels was missing, the songbirds were silent, and no
breeze stirred the colorful leaves that clung to the branches
before their lack of lifeblood severed their hold.

The quiet movements of moccasins on the forest floor
told nothing of the slow advance of shadows among the
grey and brown-barked tree trunks. Only the silence bode

something out of the ordinary. Ezra's chosen path was easier and shorter, but he would be more exposed as he faced the possible shooter head-on, and he crouched down, holding his rifle across his chest, moving his long legs like a predatory spider, and just as silently. He searched the far bank after every step before taking another, shielding himself behind the big-trunked elms and sycamores and hickories. The colors of his oily buckskins, made so by the many wipings of greasy hands, and his dark hat and skin blended well with the darkness of the woods, where light found it difficult to penetrate the thick canopy.

Gabriel moved like a cougar in the forest, each step measured, each footfall calculated and touching only after feeling through the moccasin for any twig, stone, or sound-making obstacle. But it wasn't just a silent stalk; it was the stalk of certain death for the quarry. Experienced beyond his years, the lithe blond figure slunk through the trees and undergrowth like one of its resident hunters. Quietly approaching the cover on the far bank of the creek, there was nothing that could reveal his approach except a mistake in judgment or clumsy movement. Gabriel was focused on his adversary, and with the second sense of a wise woodsman, he moved as naturally as if he had spent his entire life in such endeavors. He stopped, listening, but the only sound was the giggling trickle of the stream that came from the cavern and sought its escape down the creek bed, searching for the bigger Current River.

As each man searched, first the far bank of the creek bottom, then the area within sight of the cavern mouth, nothing was revealed. Gabriel visually scanned each cluster of brush, each rock, every tree trunk—anything and everything that would provide cover for a shooter facing the cave, but there was no movement, nothing that indicated a possible shooter. Ezra's line of sight was totally different, but neither could he see any evidence of an attacker.

Suddenly Ezra saw movement and started to bring his rifle up, but recognized Gabriel as he flitted from one tree to another, probably finding another vantage point from which to search for the shooter. Both men watched, waited, and listened. Ezra gave the quick scree of a night hawk and stepped from behind his cover, offering himself as a target for a shooter, but only for an instant. Nothing happened. No one moved or fired. The men began to relax, then heard the pounding of hooves. They looked at the low end of the finger ridge and saw the familiar figure of Long Walker astride the strawberry roan coming from the bank of the Current River at a trot.

They couldn't warn him without giving themselves away, but they readied themselves as they searched for the shooter who had smoked the cave and fired into the mouth of the cavern. But there was still no movement, and Long Walker slowed as he neared the cave, seeing the smoldering brush at the entrance. When no shots came, Ezra stepped out and hailed their friend, "Ho! Long Walker!" and started down the slope. Gabriel gave the area another quick search and, seeing nothing, he too came from the trees and approached the Indian.

Ezra explained to the Indian about the smoke and rifle fire, to which Long Walker replied, "I saw the fresh sign. One horse, run," he stood in his stirrups and turned toward the bigger river, pointing, "there, headed downstream. I could tell not your horses, so I came to see."

Every track tells a story. Whether its how fast the horse is moving or more about the horse. The length of the stride, the width of the tracks, the size of the hoof, the horseshoes and their wear, and more, so that each track is unique, and a good tracker could tell much about both the horse and its burden. Long Walker added, "I crossed this track two days back. He follows us."

"Is he one of the group that's been following us?" asked Gabriel.

"Maybe. I only see group from a distance, not tracks. They come closer."

"Did you check our backtrail last night?" asked Ezra.

"No, stayed with Quapaw."

Ezra and Gabriel looked at one another, then to Long Walker, "There doesn't happen to be a woman there you like, is there? I thought you said all the young women and older children were taken," said Gabriel, looking sideways at the man.

Long Walker scowled, "No woman. Just old people, little children."

"Did you talk to them about us helping get the captives back?" asked Gabriel.

"Yes, said we can help."

Ezra glared at his friend, "See there? Even when you ain't tryin', you manage to get us into trouble!" He grumbled as he started toward the tethered horses, "Come on, let's get it over with!"

8 / Foray

"I am Stands Alone," declared the grey-haired man. He was wrapped in a blanket that covered one shoulder and hung to the ground. His beaded moccasins showed from underneath, as did one arm and shoulder, the arm bearing a silver band above the bicep and the shoulder showing black circular tattoos. His eyes flashed at them, but it was indiscernible whether it was hatred, fear, or determination that rode on the black-eyed stare. His muscular cheeks moved with his jaw, and he spoke through gritted teeth. Behind him, work stopped as the remaining people gravitated toward the visitors led by the Tamaroa, who had shown himself to be a friend. The partially completed bark-covered lodge stood like a meatless skeleton, the only evidence of the band's willingness to rebuild what remained of their once strong people. There were others of the Quapaw that had gone farther north to join the Fox and Sauk bands, but they had remained, determined to keep to the old ways of their people.

Gabriel stepped down and, holding one rein in his left hand, he raised his right hand, open palm facing the leader, "I am Gabriel, and this," nodding toward Ezra, who now stood beside him, "is Ezra, my friend."

The leader, apparently the chief of the diminished band, looked from Gabriel to Ezra and gave a simple grunt to acknowledge the introductions, then asked, "You will go after those who took our women?" He had a scowl on his face, and distrust showed in his eyes. His clenched fist and taut jaw also showed his skepticism, but he waited for an answer.

"Our friend, Long Walker, has said this would be a good thing to do, and we agree."

"Why you do this?" asked the chief.

Ezra shuffled his feet and dropped his eyes to the ground. Catching Gabriel's attention with uplifted eyebrows and an open-handed gesture, he bid his friend explain. Gabriel turned his attention to the chief, "We want to be friends with the Quapaw, and we believe what these others have done is wrong, so we want to help."

The chief squinted at the tall young man and his dark-skinned friend with a slight snarl to his lip. He turned to Long Walker and spoke, "You go with them?"

Long Walker slowly nodded, then asked, "Will you go with us?"

The chief's expression changed; instead of suspicion, he looked at Long Walker as if he had issued a challenge. The chief dropped his blanket and reached for a quiver that rested nearby, slipped it over his shoulder and picked up his lance, "We go!"

The two friends left their packhorses in the village with the Quapaw and now rode behind Long Walker and Stands Alone. Although the Indians rode in silence, Ezra and Gabriel dropped back enough to talk as Ezra asked, "You think that old man is gonna be a help or a problem?"

Gabriel chuckled, "That old man has probably seen more than his share of battles. That lance has a handful of scalp locks, and his scars show he has fought and won. The way I understand it, most of the Plains tribes make their warriors earn the right to wear feathers. Those markings and notches on the feathers tell the story of his victories, so, I'm not gonna be the one to tell him he can't come."

Ezra nodded, then asked, "Has Long Walker said much about this war party, like how many an' such?"

"No, but he's certain we can get the captives back, so I'm willing to give it a try. Did you see the long faces on those old women in the village? They were a sad people, and I'm thinkin' we need to do this, so . . ."

"Ummhumm, and every time you get to thinkin', we get in trouble!" declared Ezra, shaking his head.

The Indians had reined up and were waiting until the two friends came alongside. Long Walker pointed to the draw below them, "They camped here first night."

"How many warriors do they have?" asked Gabriel, looking at the remnants of the camp—a fire, some branches used for bedding, droppings from the horses, and bones from a deer.

"This many, maybe more," stated Long Walker, holding up both hands with all fingers extended.

"And how many captives?"

"Six women, one girl, three boys," answered Long Walker, the chief nodding slightly as he listened.

"Is this common for the Osage?" Ezra asked the chief.

Stands Alone scowled, "These are not Osage, these are renegades. Outcasts! Their leader is Killer of Enemies, he is Osage outcast!"

"Why'd he get cast out?" asked Gabriel.

"He fought with his father, and when his mother tried to stop the fight, he killed her," explained Stands Alone. The reputation of Killer of Enemies was well known and often talked about among the different tribes and villages. He was also known to raid the villages of his own people, showing no loyalty to any tribe. Those who had gathered around him were men of similar manner and reputation, the worst of all the natives. While every tribe has its own customs and laws, all demanded respect for the leaders and elders and the rules of the tribe while giving freedom to each person to make his own choices, but when those choices endangered the people of the village or tribe, they were immediately and harshly dealt with, even to the ultimate penalty, short of death—to be cast out of the tribe and considered dead to his people.

To be isolated and alone often caused those who were outcasts to band together for survival, but the nature of the renegades did little to stop their selfish and destructive ways.

"So, these are not all Osage?" inquired Gabriel.

"There are Kickapoo, Kiowa, Kansa, Chickasaw, and others. They are growing in numbers and strength. It is said Killer of Enemies thinks he can rule this land, and will kill all those who resist. He has said the leaders of the Osage who make peace with the white trader Chouteau are betrayers of their people, and he has vowed to kill everyone who opposes him," explained Long Walker.

"How long has this Killer of Enemies been leading this band of renegades?" asked Gabriel.

"Two, three summers," answered Long Walker, looking at Stands Alone for confirmation. The old chief nodded and added, "He has destroyed three other villages of my people. Those he takes captive, he uses and destroys, keeping none alive." The chief looked at Gabriel and continued, "Killer of Enemies is a great warrior but a poor man. He is big, bigger than any man, and none can stand against him in battle. That is why he has the name 'Killer of Enemies.'"

"Oh? Just how big is he?" asked Gabriel, not sure he wanted to know.

Long Walker stepped down and motioned for Gabriel to do the same. When they were side by side, Long Walker stretched his arm high, holding his hand almost a foot above the top of Gabriel's head, "He stands this tall." Putting his hands to the sides of Gabriel's shoulders, he continued, "And his shoulders are this wide." He held his hands at least a hand's-breadth from Gabriel's shoulders.

Gabriel had craned his neck to see where Long Walker held his hand above his head, then looked at both sides when he held his hands by his shoulders, then looked at Ezra, "That's mighty big!"

"All Osage are big, this man more," added Long Walker, swinging back onto his strawberry roan mare.

"Well, from what you're saying, we've got a fight ahead of us, so, how soon do you think we can catch up?"

"After dark tomorrow," answered Long Walker and gigged his horse forward to resume their pursuit.

With a clear night, the men continued into the darkness with the big lantern of the moon to guide them. The renegades did nothing to hide their trail, obviously believing no one could or would follow. Shortly after midnight, Gabriel called for them to stop. "Our horses need some rest and graze, and so do we!" He looked to Long Walker who had returned from his scout far in front of them, and asked, "How close?"

"One day, maybe less. They are not moving fast, they will stop soon."

"Any sign of the captives?"

"Yes." Long Walker chose not to explain, which was explanation enough. When nothing was said, it was understood that what he found was not good. Probably one of the captives had been killed, and perhaps more. Gabriel chose not to press the point but busied himself tending to his big black, rubbing him down with dried grass and talking to him. The man and his horse had developed a special relationship from the first day the horse came to their home. Although sixteen, Gabriel had been going through a growing spurt, but still needed a stool to easily mount the long-legged black stallion. Now, even though the horse stood just over sixteen hands, Gabriel's growth had matched that of his horse, and he could easily swing aboard the big black. But more than that, the horse sensed the needs of his master, and Gabriel understood Ebony. Whether Gabriel called for him or simply whistled, the horse immediately responded to his call, and the big black was always watchful and sensitive to any danger to both him and his rider, and he would accept no other rider than Gabriel.

After an early start and by riding hard through the day, trying to stay in the timber and out of sight, the four pursuers made good time. Long Walker scouted ahead and came back to the edge of the thick timber to wait for the others. At his uplifted hand, they carefully drew near and listened, "They made camp. I think they plan to use the captives." His somber expression told of his concern and even hatred at the possible mistreatment of the captives.

"It is early to make camp, so something must be up," agreed Gabriel. "Where's their camp?"

At Gabriel's question, Long Walker stepped down to draw in the dirt. The others gathered around as he began. "River," he said as he drew a wide arcing line in the dirt. "Cliff, very tall, at edge of river." He pointed to the outside edge of the wide bend. "Here," he said, pointing to what would be the top of the cliff, "Many trees, all over hills." He made several brush marks showing the trees. "Here," pointing to what must be a ridge of the tall hill, "rim rock, camp below. Open, flat, then trees. Here," he pointed further from the camp, "low place between hills." He drew a line that extended to the low side of the rimrock. "Good approach, thick trees."

After he completed his crude map, he sat back on his haunches, "I will scout closer, take you." He pointed at Gabriel. "We plan attack. You," pointing to Stands Alone and Ezra, "wait here." He jabbed his stick into his drawing, indicating the end of the low draw was to be used as their approach.

Gabriel looked at Ezra and the chief, then nodded to Long Walker, "Sounds good to me." He turned back to Ezra and the chief, "We won't do anything until we come back and explain the plan. Since we're outnumbered by so many, each of us will have a big job to do to get those captives back."

The chief looked from Long Walker to Gabriel, nodded, "Yes, we wait. We all do what we must to get the women and children back or Kills His Enemies destroy them."

"I think we're all agreed on that, chief," answered Gabriel.

9 / Rimrock

They rode silently through the timber, keeping to the lowlands between the knolls. With a long ridge-like knoll between them and the camp of the renegades, they wound their way through the thick timber, moving to the apex of the draw. Long Walker stepped down, motioning to the others to follow suit. As Gabriel came to his side, he whispered and pointed, "The end of the rimrock there," then turning slightly he pointed again, "Camp there, below high point of rimrock. We go above to look down on camp." Gabriel nodded, slipped his Mongol bow from its sheath, hung the quiver over his back, and quickly strung the bow while Long Walker instructed the others to wait for his return.

Gabriel yielded to Long Walker's lead, and the two swiftly and quietly moved through the trees, climbing atop the long ridge with the rimrock. Staying away from the edge, the two trotted to the point above the camp, then dropped to their stomachs and crawled nearer the edge. The rimrock stood about thirty feet high and the camp was no more than five yards from the bottom edge of the wall, putting Gabriel and Long Walker a little less than twenty yards above the camp. With a small fire in the midst, the renegades were gathered at one end of the camp, while the captives were bound together, two by two at the opposite end. The warriors were lazing around, at least three were sleeping on their blankets, and one appeared to be standing guard, but was leaning against a tree and paying little attention to anyone or anything. Gabriel counted eleven warriors, five women, one girl, and two boys. He looked at Long Walker, "One woman and one boy are missing."

"Dead," was his response.

Gabriel crabbed back from the edge, then stood and walked toward the other end of the rimrock. He searched the top of the ridge, the cover at the edge of the rimrock, and eyeballed a way down around between the end of the rimrock and the edge of the cliff that marked the end of the knoll and the river far below. He returned to Long Walker and motioned for them to return to the others.

Once they'd returned, Gabriel smoothed a patch of dirt with his moccasin and began illustrating his plan to the others, often looking at Long Walker for his input. It was finally decided that Ezra would work his way as close as possible to the downhill side of the camp, while Long Walker and Stands Alone approached from the side where the captives were bound. Gabriel would return to the top of the rimrock and he would start the distracting attack, while the two Indians would try to grab the captives. Ezra would have them in a crossfire and would be the most vulnerable, but he showed little concern.

Once they all agreed, they picketed their horses, all but Gabriel, and started working their way to the designated positions. Gabriel reined his long-legged black through the trees and around the point of the rimrock, staying well back in the trees below the rise of the ridge to ensure that any noise would not carry over the top to the camp below the rimrock. When he thought he was about even with the camp, he stepped down and checked the loads on all his weapons, then stuffed both saddle pistols in his belt beside the over/under pistol, grabbed up his Ferguson, and started to his first firing point. He led Ebony closer to the rim, ground-tied him, and hunkered down to slowly move to his first cover. Before dropping behind the rock, he imagined his path, each point carefully calculated and each step planned. He wanted the surprise to be overwhelming and the impact to cause the renegades to believe there were many shooters.

He settled down behind the first rock, cautiously peering around and picking his first target, which was the warrior standing watch. His second would be the reclining warrior who slept soundly with his mouth wide open, snoring so loud Gabriel could hear his snorts. He waited, listening for the signal from Ezra that the others were in position. From the trees on the downhill side of the camp came the perfectly mimicked two-note trilling *tweeter-tweeter dee* of the oriole from Ezra, signaling their readiness.

Gabriel slowly eared back the hammer on his Ferguson, setting the triggers. Then, carefully taking aim and resting his finger on the back trigger, he squeezed off his shot. The big rifle roared and spat smoke and fire, sending the big lead ball into the chest of the guard, who slumped and fell. But Gabriel was on the move; running past Ebony, he slid the rifle into the scabbard and pulled one of the saddle pistols, bringing it up, hammer cocked, as he slid behind the second rock. In an instant, he brought the blade sight down on the slowly stirring sleeper and squeezed off his first shot, scoring a hit. The ball pierced the man's chest at the base of his throat, knocking him onto his back, never to wake again.

He quickly cocked the second lock, swinging the barrel toward another man who was trying to nock an arrow as he stood near a tree, but the lead ball from the second barrel of the saddle pistol entered his side and tore through the man's middle, causing him to rise on his toes and fall on his face. Gabriel jammed that pistol back in his belt as he rose to move to the next position. As he moved, he heard the blast of a rifle from below and he knew Ezra was taking a toll. The screams of the warriors were a mixture of war cries and alarm, but each one added to the confusion of the renegades.

Gabriel cocked the first lock on the second pistol, dropping to one knee beside a stunted cedar. With a different vantage point now, he spotted another warrior taking cover behind a tree close to the rimrock, but at this angle, it was an easy shot, and Gabriel sent the lead messenger of death to bury itself between the man's neck and shoulder, choking him and destroying his innards. Movement to his right caught Gabriel's attention, and he swung around to see a man bringing an arrow to bear on him. He fired too quickly for a kill shot, but it was enough to ruin the man's shot as the bullet shattered bone in his arm just behind his wrist.

Again, Gabriel rose, returned to the waiting Ebony and swung aboard, returning the saddle pistols to their holsters. He dug his heels into the black, launching him toward the end of the rimrock and the path below. Ebony responded instantly and slid with his butt dragging and front hooves digging to slow the slide down the shoulder. Gabriel pulled his over/under pistol, cocking the hammer and turning Ebony toward the tree line. He jumped down, dropping the reins to ground-tie the black, as he vaulted nearer the camp. One warrior turned at the sound, swinging his rifle toward his attacker, but he was met by the first blast of the belt pistol, causing a blossom of red on his chest. The renegade looked down as his fingers slipped from the rifle, then his knees gave way, and he crumpled into the grass.

Gabriel was on the run, rotating the barrels for the second shot. He cocked the hammer, turned to look for a target, and was hit in the middle by the shoulder of the big Osage. Killer of Enemies had charged through the trees and caught Gabriel in mid-stride, lowering his shoulder to hit him in the middle and lift him to his shoulder. With his massive arms wrapped around Gabriel, the Indian screamed his war cry, and with two long strides came to the top of the cliff. He shouted his cry again, lifted Gabriel over his head, and threw him like a ragdoll over the cliff toward the river below.

The shock of the impact had knocked the wind from

Gabriel's lungs. He tried to reach his 'hawk or his knife, but his arms were pinned to his sides. The scream of the Indian startled Gabriel, but when he was thrown through the air, he couldn't hold back his own cry of surprise. He tumbled head over heels and instantly knew he had been thrown from the cliff. He saw treetops, water, rock, and sky as he tried to control his fall, but to no avail.

Suddenly, he was crashing through branches and limbs of a tree or trees, bouncing off the bigger limbs. He tried to protect his face, but each branch grabbed and tore at him as if they were inhabited by some monster that sought his destruction. Leaves slapped at him and branches tore at him, and still he fell. A moment later he was free, then he smashed down on rocks and ground below. He tried to breathe, but only darkness came, and all was black and still.

Ezra, taking cover behind a tall oak, picked his first shot and sounded the cry of the oriole. At the opening salvo from Gabriel, Ezra squeezed off his shot and dropped the warrior nearest the captives. He snatched his over/under pistol from his belt, cocking it as he brought it up, then moved to another tree and took aim at a younger warrior who had started toward the captives. Before he could squeeze off a shot, an arrow whispered through the trees and impaled the youth, leaving nothing but the fletching showing as he fell to the ground.

Ezra picked another target, leaned against a tree to steady his aim, and squeezed off another scoring shot, taking his target just over his ear and exploding his skull in a spray of blood that caught his friend nearby. The second warrior turned quickly, searching the trees for the shooter, but was met with an arrow from Long Walker that took him under his arm and pierced his chest, causing the man to take one step and fall forward, crushing his bow beneath him.

Ezra saw the chief and Long Walker begin cutting the bonds of the captives and he turned toward the warriors, searching for anyone who might come back to the captives. But the ruckus caused by Gabriel had captured their attention, and they were fighting the ghost on the black horse as he dealt death time and again. Ezra had glanced at the captives, most now starting toward the trees, directed by Stands Alone, when suddenly he felt a blow to his hip and looked down to see an arrow protruding from his haunch. He searched for his would-be assailant and saw the warrior grabbing for the rifle dropped by a nearby renegade and Ezra snapped off a deadly shot that dropped the man on his face with a grunt.

Ezra jammed the pistol back in his belt, reached down to break off the shaft of the arrow, and limped back into the trees. He quickly reloaded his pistol and rifle, then, taking his hat and folding it up, he made a pad for the muzzle of his rifle. Standing, he used the long rifle as a crutch, butt to the ground and the padded end of the muzzle under his arm. It was a crude crutch, but he needed both his rifle and something to help him move. He started back to where the horses were picketed, knowing he had a long walk on one leg. But he would make it even if he had to crawl.

10 / Recovery

Every step sent bolts of pain shooting down his leg and up his side. Blood still oozed from the wound, and he struggled to take each step. He knew he was losing too much blood and would probably pass out before reaching the horses, if the others even left his horse behind. He stumbled and fell, tripping over his own feet but protecting his rifle as he tumbled to the ground. He groaned and pulled himself up to sit leaning against a tree. Looking down at the stub of the arrow, Ezra saw his hip and pants leg soaked with blood.

He cautiously touched the shaft, gritted his teeth, and held his breath against the pain. When he jerked it, he discovered the arrowhead was apparently lodged in a bone. Unable to extract it, he fell back against the tree, breathing deeply, and looked around for anything to stanch the flow of blood. Thinking he heard something, he caught his breath and pulled his rifle across his legs, quickly checking the load and slowly earing back the hammer to set the trigger. There it was again—the soft tread of something moving through the trees. He listened, drawing back as close to the tree trunk as possible. The steps were irregular, but he could make out more than just one person. It was either a four-legged beast or two people, and he was thinking it was two people. Then he saw movement and bending down, he saw the legs of two, the first with long fringed leggings over moccasins, and the second bare-legged with moccasins. He slowly raised his rifle to his shoulder, waiting for the two to come closer or at least give him a clear shot.

Then he heard the *tweeter tweeter dee* of the oriole call, the same call he'd used to signal Gabriel, but he knew that wasn't Gabriel since his buckskins had no fringe on the legs. He hesitated for a moment, then answered the call with one of his own, and the legs again came toward him. He lifted his rifle, finger on the thin rear trigger, drew in a breath and let a little out, then waited. As the figures neared, he slowly tightened his squeeze on the trigger, but the whispered, "Gabriel?" stopped him. He let out his breath, relieved, and answered, "No, Ezra!"

Long Walker stepped from the trees, followed by a woman holding a bow with an arrow nocked. Long Walker carried his lance, and Ezra recognized the quiver of arrows at the waist of the woman as the Tamaroa's. He came to Ezra's side and looked at the wound, "In bone?"

Ezra nodded, "I was looking for something to stop the bleeding before I started out again."

Long Walker said, "This Pale Otter, good with that," and nodded toward the wound. He looked at the woman, "You fix him. I will come back."

She looked from Walker to Ezra, nodded, and handed off the bow and quiver. Without a word to Ezra, she started into the trees, looking for what she would need. Within a few moments, she returned with an arm full of plants that she dropped beside Ezra. She knelt and stripped the bark from a couple of willow twigs, then demonstrated to Ezra that he should chew on the bark. He nodded, put a couple pieces in his mouth, and started chewing. She grabbed a couple of stones, one larger and somewhat flat, then started grinding and mashing the plants into a poultice.

As she worked, Ezra watched, thinking he recognized a couple of the plants as bee balm and cornflower, but there was at least one other he didn't recognize. He looked at the woman and scanned her features. She was pretty, with a single long braid hanging down her back, a wide forehead over thin eyebrows, and eyes that showed concentration and compassion. Her triangle-shaped face with its pouty lips and petite nose was well proportioned and attractive. Her buckskin dress had minimal beading, and it fit her curves quite well. He smiled at his deduction that she was quite pretty but erased his expression when she looked up at him and glared as she motioned for him to chew on the willow bark. He nodded, took another portion, and started chewing more of the thin strips. As he thought about it, he realized the pain in his hip had lessened, probably because of the willow.

When she finished her poultice, she made him stretch out and roll onto his right side, giving her access to the wound. She used his knife to cut away the buckskins, then paused and started cutting off the leg of the britches, to the protest of Ezra, but her scowling look stayed his protest and he cradled his head on his bent right arm as she continued. She slipped the knife scabbard from his belt and held it to his mouth, motioning for him to put it between his teeth, indicating she was going to cut out the arrow. He no sooner had the leather between his teeth when he felt the jabbing, searing pain as she cut into the wound. He bit into the leather to stifle a scream and tensed every muscle in his body, then he slowly let out his air as he dropped into unconsciousness.

Rhythmic plodding and thudding pain brought Ezra awake. He saw the mane and head of the horse before him and felt the binding on his ankles that kept him on the horse, but was surprised to feel the woman behind him with her arms around his waist, holding him secure. He looked around just enough to know they were on a trail in the woods, then he lapsed back into the black void of nothingness. When next he woke, he was lying on his back, covered with a blanket, and looking up at the skeleton of a bark-covered lodge overhead. He looked around, seeing other blankets and robes arrayed throughout the interior, along with some parfleches, a quiver of arrows, a couple of lances, and some clothing made of buckskin. He looked down at his bare chest, then lifted the blanket and saw only a wide bandage at his hip, and no other clothing. His eyebrows raised, he lowered the blanket and grabbed another to put under his head, then laid back down. He was weak, but the pain seemed less, and he knew he would heal, but his mind began racing with questions. Just then, the blanket at the doorway was pushed back and the woman who had worked on him in the woods walked into the lodge, a smile painting her face when she saw that Ezra was awake.

She knelt beside him, sat back on her heels, and began talking in French or some semblance of it, only to be stopped by Ezra with an upheld hand. He shook his head, "English, I don't know much French. A little Spanish, but that's all."

She frowned, then, smiling, she stood and left the lodge, returning in a couple of moments with another woman behind her. The older woman remained standing when Otter resumed her place beside Ezra and said, "I speak English." Then pointing at Otter, she said, "She wants to know how you feel? Any pain?"

"Uh, well, I guess I feel good. A little weak, but not too much pain," he answered, scowling slightly. "But I need to know about my friend, Gabriel. Is he here?"

Otter frowned and looked at the older woman as she translated then rattled off some response, which was quickly interpreted as, "Your friend is not here. Long Walker went looking for him but has not returned."

"How long have I been here?" asked Ezra, alarmed.

"Two days," came the answer.

He frowned, thought about it, and mumbled, "Two days' travel, two days here. Where is he? I've got to get up and go find him!" He threw back the covers, startling Otter and the interpreter, but when he tried to stand, he realized he was unclothed, and the pain in his hip forced him back to the blankets. After covering his embarrassment, he asked, "How soon? How soon will I be able to ride?"

Otter held up three, then four fingers, cocking her head to the side to indicate uncertainty. She spoke again, and the interpreter said, "She will change your bandage, so be still while she works." Otter tossed the blanket aside, giggled as Ezra grabbed at it to cover himself, then, with a serious expression but with a smile tugging at the corners of her mouth, she began removing the bandage and poultice.

*   *   *   *   *

It was mud. Mud and silt and rocks. With one eye open, Gabriel could see his fingers move under the silt as he tried to pull his hand toward him. The sunlight bounced off the rippling waters of the Gasconade River, making him squint to see. He breathed deep, tasting mud on his lips and wincing from the stabbing pain in his side. He choked, coughed, moaned from the pain, and tried to get his hands and knees under him. The water permeated his buckskin britches, what was left of them. Once up on his hands, he looked at his chest to see the tunic hanging in shreds to the mud below. The strap of the quiver crossed his chest, and he felt the taut strip of leather binding his tunic. He sucked in a deep breath, wincing again as he did a mental check of his body, believing that every limb and every portion of his body hurt. Pulling his hands from the sucking mud, he rolled to the side and sat up, stretching his legs before him, his feet in the water. Scratches and cuts, some still bleeding, showed through the shreds of buckskin and covered his legs and arms. He felt over his body for any indication of broken bones, concluding that the only things broken were a couple of ribs. He put his hand to his face, where he felt a strip of skin hanging from the side of his head, and fingered the deep cut that had torn loose a strip of his scalp. He looked around, searching for anything that would tell him where he was and what there was that might help his condition.

Before him, the river made a wide bend, splashing against the sandbar below him and moving away to the south. Behind him rose a granite cliff, towering more than two hundred feet overhead, with just a couple of tufts of brush clinging to meager crevices. On the narrow bank beside him and resting in the shade of the cliff was a cluster of dogwood showing red and yellow and two towering ash trees with thick crowns of bright yellow. A smaller sycamore stood alone with its mottled trunk and big leaves, now brown and gold, struggling to keep their grip just a little longer. Based on where he sat, Gabriel surmised it was because of the thick leaves of the big ash tree that he'd survived the fall, but the tree had taken its toll on him, protesting his fall with every branch and twig that clawed at him as he fell.

He staggered to his feet, looking around for anything useful. He spotted a pair of arrows that had fallen from his quiver, picked them up and looked for his bow and more arrows. He found a half-dozen more arrows and his toma-hawk, and felt for the knife that usually rested in its sheath on a sling between his shoulder blades. He was relieved to feel it still in place. He continued his search for the bow, and finally saw it hanging on a branch about fifteen feet off the ground high up in the golden ash tree. With a heavy breath of determination, he started his climb, and after slipping a couple of times with his wet moccasins, he finally retrieved the bow, relieved to find it undamaged.

Back on the ground, he stepped away from the cliff and lifted his eyes to search the face of the granite monolith for a possible way to the top. Seeing none, he scanned the wide bend at the base for a possible route around and, seeing the only possibility to be at the left end, he looked down at himself and his clothing to prepare himself for the trek. But first, he needed to give some attention to the worst of the cuts, and maybe bind his chest to support the broken ribs. He looked around, then walked through the trees and brush, cut some branches of willow, and searched the shoreline, hoping for something that might have washed up. He had gone no more than ten yards along the waterline when his eyes caught something shiny. Bending down to examine it, he was pleased to find his over/under pistol partially buried in the mud, but otherwise intact. Not that it would do him any good, since the powder horn and possibles bag with the balls was hanging on the pommel of his saddle somewhere in the woods above the cliff.

11 / Reunion

There was no way around the cliff face that stretched the length of the bend in the river. Upstream, the river piled water against the cliff face before yielding to the force behind it and bending to the south, having washed eons of mud, silt, and driftwood to pile against the face to give a toehold for the trees to grow tall, holding the soil with deep-diving roots. Downstream where the force of the water had valiantly pushed against the limestone, only to find it unyielding, it carried everything, soil, sand, and seed, around the point to find a landing place further on downstream.

Once Gabriel discovered he was marooned on the half-moon sandbank with no way to climb the towering cliff face, he turned his attention to other possibilities. He stood at the edge of the water, watching the current twist and turn as it passed his feet. Getting an idea, he turned back to the pile of grey driftwood. He stood staring at the stack, knowing he needed something to bind his wounds, food, warmth, and weapons. He had the bow and arrows, but water would ruin the laminate, the horn, wood, and sinew that were held together with animal glue. He was losing strength from the loss of blood, and time was his enemy. With another look around, he began work on his plan.

He stripped off his buckskins, laying the ragged tunic flat. The pile of big and somewhat sticky sycamore leaves was used as a carpet upon the tunic. He laid the unstrung Mongol Bow and quiver of arrows on the leaves, then wrapped the bundle tightly, pushing it into one leg of the britches. The second leg had been cut into strips that were used to tightly bind the bundle and secure it to the topside of a large driftwood log. Gabriel was a strong swimmer, and he was confident in his ability to make the bend and the rapids, but his concern was the weapons.

He studied the current and moved the log and bundle to the high side of the bend, then pushed it into the backwater of the river. Holding tightly to the buckskin strips and the log, he lunged forward, pushing the log into the stronger current. He stretched out behind the narrow raft, kicking and pushing the log, trying for the edge of the current that was forced away from the cliff face. Water splashed his face and he gasped for air, gripping the stub of a branch on the log that was his handhold, kicking to force the log to his will. Again, and again the rapids crashed over the log, taking him full in the face, catching him as he struggled for air and filling his mouth. He spat, sucked air, kicked and pushed, feeling the current bend as it forced its way past the cliff face. Now was the most difficult part, where the water twisted like a rope, turning upon itself and dragging surface debris under, but Gabriel pushed and kicked, using one arm to paddle. He tugged on the stub of branch, felt it give way, and fought to catch the log as the strong current wrenched it from his grasp.

White water splashed and tugged against him as he fought for air. Seeing the cliff face rushing toward him, he reached out and dug deep with one arm, then the other, kicking frantically, digging into the water and fighting, briefly glimpsing the log as it was pulled away. As he was fighting for his life in the strong current, his foot struck a rock, scraping skin and breaking his stroke. He turned to his side and again stretched for a deeper draw, pulled himself to the edge of the current, then as the river cascaded around the edge of the cliff, he was pulled under, tumbling, fighting, kicking, unable to breathe. His eyes open, he saw bubbles, white water, debris, rocks, and still he fought, unable to determine the surface from the rapids. Then air, blessed air, and smooth water. He looked to see the log less than ten feet away, gently rocking on the smooth water, bundle still on top. He kicked over to it, latched on, and dragged it to shore to pull it up just enough for him to drop to the sand and gasp for air, turning over to face the sun and basking in the warmth.

He sat up, looking at his naked body and the obvious wounds. The scrape on his foot and shin was nasty but not too bad. *That's gonna leave a bruise!* he thought. Then, feeling the gouge on his scalp, his hand came back bloody. Another long cut on his left thigh was bleeding and one on his right forearm showed fresh blood, but the rest of the scrapes, scratches, and cuts from his fall, now cleansed by his swim, showed little fresh blood. He was relieved, knowing they would heal quickly. But the others would need attention.

He reached for the bundle with his bow and untied it, keeping the leather strips, and was pleased to see the minimal moisture within. He knew his bow and pistol were undamaged. He retrieved his moccasins, fashioned a breechcloth from the buckskin, and kept the remaining bits to use for bandaging his wounds once he found what he needed for some poultices.

After a quick survey of his surroundings, he moved into the trees, strung his bow, and planned his route as he walked, wanting to first return to the renegade campsite and hopefully find Ebony. He was confident the horse would not allow himself to be taken by another, but he might not stay nearby and could be wandering the wilderness on his own or in pursuit of other horses. He was a stallion and could be misled by a mare in season. Gabriel chuckled at the thought, then let out with the whistle he often used to summon the horse. He waited, listening, but there was nothing other than the usual sounds of the forest, a chattering squirrel that scolded him for invading his territory, a circling falcon that gave his echoing call, and the creak of deadwood rubbing against other still-standing trunks.

As he climbed the backside of the hill with the rimrock, he spotted some goldenrod and snatched up a handful, a little further on, some plantain caught his eye, and he grabbed some on his way through the thicket. He looked at the cut on his thigh and the wound on his forearm, then felt the gouge in his scalp and stopped under a big oak, seating himself on a pile of freshly fallen leaves. He picked up a couple of rocks and began making a poultice of the leaves and roots of the plants.

In short order, his thigh, arm, and head were sporting bandages of poultices covered by patches of buckskin, held in place by strips of the same buckskin. He was pleased with his handiwork but uncomfortable with the one on his head, held in place with a strip of buckskin that went under his chin and was tied with a knot next to his ear. He thought he must look like a girl on her way to church with a new bonnet on her head, but at least the wounds were clean and covered and the blood flow was stanched. He stood and started off again, cautiously watching for any sign of the renegades or his horse.

As he neared the crest of the hill and the end of the rim-rock, he was on familiar ground, and whistled for Ebony again. Still no response. He walked through the thinning trees to the edge of the rimrock, then started along the same route he had taken before the big Osage caught him and gave him a flying lesson. After a few moments, he heard something that caused him to stop beside a big oak and nock an arrow. A shadow moved, then Ebony stepped into the clear, ears forward as he looked directly at Gabriel. One rein trailing, he was no more than twenty yards from where he had been ground-tied the day before. Gabriel grinned, replaced the arrow in his quiver, and walked to Ebony. Hand outstretched, he spoke softly to his friend, who stepped back as he looked at Gabriel. He recognized the voice, but not having seen Gabriel in the buff before and looking very white, he wasn't too certain of his friend. But he stood waiting, and when Gabriel came near and spoke, then scratched his head, he pushed back and accepted the attention.

Gabriel checked his gear, saw the stock of the Ferguson, the butts of the saddle pistols, and his horn and bag hanging at the pommel. He stripped the gear from the stallion and dropped it to the ground, then, grabbing a handful of grass, he gave the faithful friend a good rubdown, talking all the while. Then he took the time to clean and reload all his weapons, returning the over/under to his belt and the others to the holsters before saddling Ebony.

He mounted up and started down the narrow pass between the rimrock and the cliff, watchful for any sign of the renegades, but believing those who survived, if any, were long gone. Buzzards, crows, coyotes, a badger, and a wolverine were busy at the carcasses of the dead renegades. Often scrapping with one another, they paid no attention to Gabriel as he sat at the edge of the clearing. He searched nearby and saw the tracks of three horses headed southeast down the face of the timbered hill, believing these were the rest of the renegades.

With no sign of the captives nor his friends, Gabriel reined Ebony toward the place where the others had picketed their horses. Once there, he stepped down to check the tracks and saw where all the horses and more, probably those taken from the renegades, had gathered and headed back to the village. He mounted up to follow, lifting his eyes to the sun and calculating how much daylight was left for his travels.

* * * * *

"I found 'em! Him an' the negra! They's got a Injun with 'em too!" declared Ledbetter as he stood by the cookfire. Frenchy and Frank sat across the fire and listened to the report of their scout.

"An' just where'd you find 'em?" asked Frank, anxious for revenge on the first man who'd ever bested him in a fight.

"Bout a day's ride north. They were in a cave of sorts 'til I smoked 'em out!"

Frank jumped to his feet, "I tol' you not to spook 'em!" he shouted, shaking a finger at the scout.

"I didn't spook 'em. You said slow 'em down if I could, an' I figgered to maybe wound 'em or scare 'em. But they got out and I left, but when I circled back, I saw 'em goin' into a Injun village."

"An Injun village? What fer?" growled Frank.

"How should I know? They just did, that's all. Prob'ly cuz o' that injun that was with 'em."

"We ain't prepared to take on a whole village!" interjected Frenchy. "How 'bout we have Bucky scout it out 'n watch for 'em to leave? We can move a little closer and wait till the odds are more in our favor."

Frank sat back down, thinking, then nodded, "Yeah, good thinkin', Frenchy. We'll all move a little closer. That way, Bucky'll know where we are, an' he can come tell us as soon as they leave the village."

"But what if they decide to winter with them Injuns? I knowed fellas to find a nice warm squaw an' hol' up all winter!" whined the weasel known as Squirrel.

"You let those of us what knows how do the thinkin'!" scolded Frank, "'sides, they ain't been with them Injuns long 'nuff to get some squaw to let 'em in her lodge." He looked around at the others then added, "Get some sleep. We're movin' out first thing in the mornin'!"

12 / Village

They met on the trail. The usually stoic Long Walker grinned as he rode his horse around Ebony, looking at the near-naked figure in the saddle showing an abundance of white skin, unlike any Long Walker had ever seen. He chuckled and smiled as he looked at his friend, "White man."

Gabriel tried to keep from laughing but failed, and, shaking his head, he said, "All right. You've had your look, now let's get to the village."

Long Walker led the way but shortly reined up atop a slight knoll that offered a good view of the rolling hills that banked the Gasconade River. He lifted his arm and pointed to the distant valley, "Those that follow wait there."

Gabriel looked at Long Walker, surprise showing, and then in the direction he pointed. There was nothing to indicate a camp, no smoke, no clearing, nothing. "You have seen them?"

He nodded without speaking.

"How many?" asked Gabriel.

"This many!" He held out one hand with all fingers extended, "and another that scouts. One ver' big, one not so, one looks like a weasel, two more."

"The big one…was his arm bandaged, or in a sling like this?" He demonstrated with his arm held close to his chest.

"Yes."

"And you say they're waiting? How long have they been there?"

"Yes, wait. One night, one day, but not leaving," answered Long Walker.

"Well, if they're waiting for me, I don't want to bring them to the village of the Quapaw. Maybe I better not go there." Then he looked down at his bare legs and added, "But I need to get some buckskins. You think there's anyone in the village who can make me a pair?"

"Yes. Women who were captive can and many older women glad to make. Village has more now. Some warriors hunt when renegades attacked now back. Women make many lodges."

"And Ezra? You said he was hit with an arrow. He all right?"

Long Walker chuckled, "Yes, but good woman take care of him. He maybe stay long time."

"Oh, so it's a woman who's got him layin' abed, is it? I shoulda known!"

They waited till after dark had settled in before they approached the village. Using the trees as cover, they led their horses quietly into the camp after being confronted by one of the warriors, who let them pass. But the approach of Long Walker, followed by Gabriel, did not go unnoticed. The very white man caused a stir among those who tended the cook-fires or worked on the lodges by torchlight. Everyone turned to look, some gasping and drawing back since he resembled the image often spoken of in their tales of the ancients. But others pointed, snickered, and outright laughed while Gabriel hung his head, unable to cover the whiteness of skin that had never before seen sunlight.

The lodge that housed Ezra was pointed out and Gabriel tethered Ebony beside the bark covered lodge. When he scratched at the door, he was met by Pale Otter, who motioned him inside. She put her hand to her mouth, trying to keep from snickering as he passed, but she failed, much to the delight of Ezra, now propped up on his blankets.

"There you are," then chuckling, he added, "White man! No wonder the women are laughing. Even in the moonlight, you must look like a ghost to them! And that bonnet! Wouldn't those high-society women like to see you now!"

"All right, all right, enough laughing at my expense, even though it *is* kinda funny. I can just imagine walking into one of those fancy dances looking like this!" he commented, laughing at himself. "But, it's good to see you lookin' so well." He turned to Pale Otter, "and under such attentive care!"

It was Ezra's turn to take a ribbing, but he grinned and

said, "You can't blame me for wanting a little of the attention you always seem to get!"

"Oh, I don't. But we've got a bigger problem," replied the now-somber Gabriel. "Those men who were following us? They're not too far away, and I think they know we're here. In the village, I mean."

"You think they're some more of the bounty hunters?" asked Ezra, sitting up straighter and leaning toward his friend, who had seated himself nearby.

"That's all I can figure. I can't imagine that Frank character would be so vengeful as to follow us all this way, but who knows?"

"You remember that old man who was talkin' in the livery when we were waiting on the smithy? Didn't he say that Frank and his men were known to go with some river pirates? And what if some of those pirates we fought on the Ohio happened to come to New Madrid and let ol' Frank know about the bounty?"

Gabriel stared at his friend, dropped his eyes, and considered, "I guess it's possible, 'cause some of those on the keelboat did get away."

"Ummhumm, and I'd be willin' to bet the others with ol' Frank is some of those same pirates that wanted your head back on the river," surmised Ezra.

"Makes sense, I reckon. Well, I've got to get me some buckskins 'fore I go anywhere. Long Walker said he'd find one of the old women to fix me up with a set or two. Do you have our packs in here?" he asked, looking around. "I've got another set that Delaware woman made for us back in Pittsburgh, but I still need at least one more set."

"By all means, get some clothes on 'fore you make these people think they've been invaded by ghosts!" declared Ezra, laughing.

The old woman who had translated for Ezra came into the lodge, gave a cursory glance to Ezra and Gabriel, and spoke to Otter in her tongue. The young woman smiled, responded, and looked to Gabriel. The old woman spoke, "She said I am to tell you my name. I am known as Tinogkukquas, Bird or Mockingbird, because I speak different languages. I will help Otter tend to you." She pointed at Gabriel, "now you lay on blankets, and I will fix your bandages." She spoke with authority and started toward Gabriel with an expression that reminded him of his mother when he was young. Without saying a word, he rolled to the blankets and stretched out, arms folded behind his head as Ezra and Otter chuckled as they watched.

Bird quickly removed the bandages and poultices, nodding as she looked at the poultices, undoubtedly recognizing the plant mixture. With a glance to Gabriel, she finished removing the other bandages. She scooted around toward his head to examine the gouge in his scalp and tenderly touched it, then snatched Gabriel's knife from his scabbard and cut the dangling piece of scalp with one swipe, eliciting a wince from him. He looked at Ezra, "That's the first time I've been scalped by a woman!"

Bird laughed and translated for Otter, and both women giggled at the remark. Bird used Otter's makings and paraphernalia to clean and bandage Gabriel's wounds and soon stood and nodded her head in satisfaction before directing him to stand. Gabriel frowned but obeyed, and the woman pulled a cord from her pocket and began measuring him for new buckskins and moccasins. He lifted his arms, stretched out his legs, and stood as still as possible as she poked and prodded. He sat down when she'd finished.

Long Walker and Stands Alone came in the lodge, greeted the men, and sat down across from the pair of friends. Long Walker began, "We know men who follow you are near, but they not move. Scout for them watches the village, but I not know if he sees you," he said, nodding at Gabriel. "You," pointing with his chin to Ezra, "here before they come."

"When you told me about those men and the big man with the bad arm, I knew who they are, and they *are* after me," explained Gabriel. "I do not want to bring this on your people, so I will leave. If it is all right with you," he nodded to Stands Alone, "I will stay this night and tomorrow, but will leave tomorrow night."

Long Walker looked at Stands Alone, and the old chief began, "We did not come to tell you to leave, we came to say we will fight with you. You did much for our people to bring back the captives, and we must help you."

"Chief, I am honored that you would do this, but your people have suffered much already. Winter is coming, and you have plenty to do to ready your village for the cold. You don't need to be getting involved in a fight that is not yours. I will leave and these men will follow, and your people will not be involved."

Ezra spoke in a low voice, "I'm not sure I'll be ready by tomorrow night. It wasn't just takin' an arrow. It was stuck in the bone, and she," he nodded at Otter, "had to cut it out. That was worse than the arrow wound. But no matter what, you ain't leavin' me behind!"

"How can we help?" asked Long Walker.

"I dunno right off, Long Walker, but let me think on it and there might be a way. I ain't anxious to meet up with these fellas, and if I can figger a way to get gone from here without them knowin' it, then that's what I'll do. But right now, I don't know. If you have any ideas, let me know."

"*Wab wàwàckèci,* you are a friend of the Quapaw," stated Stands Alone as he rose to leave. Gabriel also stood, extended his arm to clasp forearms with the chief, and watched as he and Long Walker left the lodge. He sat back down and asked Bird, "What'd he call me?"

"'White Cougar.' It is an honor to receive a name from the chief. He told the others you fought like a lion, and after seeing you this night . . ." she laughed and pointed at his white legs, and the others joined in the laughter. It felt good to laugh and Gabriel tried to remember the last time he had enjoyed the laughter of others as well as his own, but nothing came to mind. It had been far too long, and it would probably be much longer before they laughed again.

13 / Getaway

Bird held out the bundle to Gabriel and explained, "These were my man's. I fixed them for you. He was a good man, but the renegades killed him in the attack."

Gabriel accepted the bundle, "I am honored, Mockingbird. And I thank you." He unfolded the top, saw the two bands of beading that stretched over the shoulders, and looked at Bird, "These are excellent! You do good work." He had selected some of the trade goods they'd purchased in Pittsburgh and New Madrid and handed her the small bundle that contained a metal mirror, a comb and brush, a tin of vermillion, and some trade beads. In any usual trade among the native tribes, this would be considered a fortune, and Bird's eyes flared wide. She looked from the goods to Gabriel, and he saw tears forming and start down her cheek. She was speechless, and turned away to leave before she got more embarrassed.

"I think she liked that, don't you?" asked Ezra. He was

standing and putting his hip to the test, wincing with every step, but walking around the inside of the bark lodge.

"Yeah, she did. But this is a fine set, good soft buckskin, and that beadwork is impressive," replied Gabriel. He had finished packing the panniers and parfleches for the pack-horses and stood looking around the lodge to be sure he wasn't forgetting anything. His saddle rested near the entry, and he knelt on one knee to check the weapons. He was especially concerned about the Mongol bow, knowing that any moisture could do serious damage. His swim in the river had gotten just about everything wet, although the bow had been well wrapped. He examined the horn belly and the birchbark covering and was satisfied it was sound and undamaged. He replaced the bow in its scabbard and stood to face Ezra, "The way you're limping around, do you think you should be trying to ride? I don't plan on taking it easy. I think moving fast at night would be the best, and it won't be laid-back."

"You ain't gettin' rid of me like that! 'Sides, I ain't walkin', I'm ridin'! And you ain't all that healthy, bein' scalped by a woman an' all!" declared Ezra.

Gabriel had to chuckle at his remark and gave in to the entreaty of his friend. He was relieved since he really didn't want to undertake this journey alone. Ezra had always been at his side and the two were like brothers, always watching each other's back. Gabriel bent to look out the entry, checking the remaining daylight, but not wanting to show himself to any watcher. He saw Long Walker approaching and stepped back to admit the Tamaroa. Long Walker glanced at

Ezra, then spoke to Gabriel, "The scout of men who follow was on hill," nodding his head behind him to the larger hill that shaded the village. "He is gone."

"Good, but we'll wait till dark to leave anyway."

They had spoken earlier in the day and Long Walker had said he would go with them, but he wanted to stay with the Quapaw. "The woman, Mockingbird, needs a man in her lodge. It would be good to have a people again."

"And they could use another good warrior, Long Walker. It would be good for you to have a family and a people, and you have been a special friend to us," answered Gabriel.

"I scout but return before you go," stated Long Walker as he turned to leave the lodge. Bird came in as he was leaving and they spoke briefly before she turned to Gabriel, "Little Badger and his friend will bring your horses as soon as it is dark, as you asked."

"Thank you, Bird. I am happy for you and Long Walker. He is a good man," said Gabriel.

Bird dropped her eyes and answered softly, "Yes, he is a good man, but he is not Quapaw."

Gabriel grinned, "But he is a good warrior, and you can make him a part of your village and your people. You can make him a good Quapaw."

She smiled and nodded, then started to leave, but turned back and gave Gabriel a big hug, nodded to Ezra, and quickly left the lodge.

With the north star off his right shoulder, Gabriel led the way as both he and Ezra trailed a loaded packhorse. The timber was thick, and the warmth of Indian summer gave the trees added incentive to hold onto their leaves, while the big moon splashed its silvery shine on the multitude of colors around them. Gabriel had always enjoyed moonlit nights, and to travel with the stars as their guide believing it was the epitome of fulfillment for their journey. With the only sounds the creak of leather, the rattle of hooves on an occasional stone, the crunch of dried leaves under hoof, and the random question of a great horned owl from the shadows, it was an enjoyable night. Although both men rode silently, they were taking in their surroundings and the experience, logging it in their mental journal of memories.

The night passed quickly and they made good time, covering what Gabriel estimated to be close to twenty miles, stopping only once to give the horses a blow and to take some jerky themselves. They continued to put miles behind them, but in the darkest moments of night, just before dawn, something stirred in the shadows of the trees, and Gabriel reined up to watch and listen.

A low moan came from near a cluster of dogwood, unlike any animal sound, and both men guessed it to be a man. Ezra whispered, "Could be a trap!" As they sat and listened, a packhorse stepped forward and blew, but no other sound came. "I dunno," answered Gabriel, "but I'm gonna check it out." He handed the reins of Ebony to Ezra, swung his leg over the rump of the black, and slowly stepped to the ground.

He eared back the hammer on his over/under as he held it waist-high, and in a slight crouch, picked his way slowly through the brush, making for the dogwood where the sound had originated. With each step carefully chosen, testing the leaves and more beneath his moccasins, he moved into the shadows. He heard ragged breathing coming from the base of the clump of dogwood. He dropped to one knee, pushing aside the near brush, searching the darkness for movement. A low moan, barely perceptible, came with the rustle of leaves, no more than a scurrying field mouse, but this was no mouse. Gabriel saw the glint of a blade that flashed in the moonlight and he rolled to the side, the knife clattering through the brush and the rocks.

He came to his feet and spoke, "Is that any way to greet a fella?"

Another groan, but now nearer. Gabriel detected something amiss. This wasn't a man, this was a woman—an Indian woman! He dropped to one knee and tried a few words of the Algonquin dialect, but no answer came. The breathing was still ragged but steady. He moved closer, pistol ready, and could better make out the form that did not move. He stretched out his hand and touched her arm, but she did not respond. He spoke again, but no response came. Stuffing his pistol in his belt, he reached out with both hands and drew the woman near, then lifted her and started back to the horses with her in his arms.

As he neared Ezra, he spoke, "Let's make camp here, good a place as any, and there's somebody here that needs some doctorin'."

"What?!" asked Ezra somewhat incredulously and leaned forward to eye his friend as he approached with his burden. "Who you got there?"

"A woman! And she's hurt."

"A woman?" He shrugged, chuckling, "Only you . . ." and he stepped down to start making camp.

They made a small fire under the long limbs of a maple, shielded from view by their stacked packs and other gear, and stretched the woman out on a blanket nearby. Gabriel had checked her over and found an arrow wound in her back, but either the arrow had fallen out or been pulled out. The rest were scratches and minor cuts from crawling or running through brush. He cleaned her wound, made a poultice and applied a bandage to hold it, and sat back, "That's 'bout all we can do, at least until she comes to. She's lost blood, and she's got some bruises an' such, so I don't know if she was beaten or what. We'll just have to wait." He looked at Ezra, "That coffee ready?"

"Ummhmm, but tell me, what're we gonna do with her?"

"I dunno, but we can't just leave her, can we?"

"No, I reckon not, but lest you forget, we have our own troubles, and we don't know how soon they catch up with us," he mulled, poking at the hot coals with a stick, sending a shower of sparks into the branches above them.

"Well, that trouble is comin' whether we help her or not. But . . ."

"I know, I know, another damsel in distress and you're still thinkin' you're one o' those knights in shining armor! So, what does that make me, your squire?" laughed Ezra.

"No, that makes us both knights! I'm the white knight . . ."

"And I'm the black knight! But wait a minute... In all the stories we read, the black knight was a bad guy!"

They both chuckled, sipping their coffee and watching as the dim light of morning dappled the woods around them. Tired from the long night of travel, they preferred sleep to eating, so they rolled out their blankets, and with one last check of the woman, they turned in for some rest.

14 / Recruit

The smell of frying meat brought Gabriel instantly awake. Without moving, he looked around the campsite and saw Ezra sitting on the log and the woman busy at the fire. Several strips of fresh meat were dangling over the low flames, dripping juice into the fire. The coffee pot sat idly by on a hot stone, and Ezra grinned at Gabriel as he began to move. Sitting up, he stretched and looked at the sky to judge the time, thinking it to be mid to late afternoon. His stomach growled as he smelled the meat and saw some Indian potatoes in the coals.

He looked up as Ezra said, "Afternoon, sleepyhead. Let me introduce to Honey Bear, a proud member of the Osage people."

"'Honey Bear?' Is that her name or your nickname?"

"It is my name," answered the woman, "In my tongue, it is Amomakwa, but I am not like the honey bear of the woods. My mother's brother gave me the name because when I was small, I chased a bear away from a beehive because I wanted the honey." Her eyes glazed over as she remembered the time with her uncle, then she pushed the potatoes farther into the coals, not yet looking directly at Gabriel.

Gabriel looked askance toward Ezra, and he answered the unspoken question, "Yeah, I know. She woke me up too. But that food sure smells mighty fine, wouldn't you say?"

Gabriel rolled from his blankets, stood, stretched, then looked down at the woman, "Are your people nearby?"

"I do not know. When I was taken by the Pawnee, the camp was by the Niangua River, but they have moved, maybe to the fort."

"How long were you with the Pawnee?" asked Gabriel

"Two moons, and I escape. One man want me for his woman. He come after me, but I kill him."

"Is he the one that put the arrow in your back?"

"Yes," she answered stoically.

"Why didn't you run away from us?" asked Ezra.

"I was not bound. My back was bandaged. You did not hurt me, you helped me. Why would I run?" She looked from one to the other, then at the meat, "It is ready."

Both men set to on the food, and wasted little time or effort downing the tasty potatoes, an unusual treat for the men. The entire meal was savory and memorable. They sat back, wiped their hands on their buckskins and looked at Bear as she finished her portion, eating with manners that would be suitable in any civilized town. Gabriel frowned and asked, "So, where did you learn English and to eat with manners like that?" nodding at her as she used some inner bark stripping to wipe her hands.

"The black robes came to my village long ago, when I was very young. They taught us about your Jesus and to speak French and English, and how to act like a white man. They were with us for many summers but left before the Spanish came," she explained. Gabriel knew the French had many Jesuit missionary priests who came from the Canadian territories south through Fort Michilimackinac and Detroit, even after the French surrendered much of their lands to the British following the Seven Years War.

"What do you plan to do now?" asked Gabriel.

"I must find my people. They must know what happened to our war party."

"*Your* war party? I thought you were taken by the Pawnees?"

"Yes. When our warriors attacked the Pawnee after they attacked our village, it was to rescue the captives. But we were defeated, and the other warriors were killed. I alone lived."

"You mean, you were with the warriors when they attacked?" asked Gabriel skeptically.

Bear straightened up, stiffening her back and lifting her head, one hand on the knife in her belt, "I am a warrior of the Ni-u-kon-ska people!"

"But I thought all the warriors of the Osage shaved their heads, except for that roach at the back?" suggested Gabriel, pointing at her hair, which hung loosely down her back.

"I am a woman, and our hair is our crown! Your Bible teaches that! But these," she pushed her hair back, revealing heavily adorned ears, the lobes cut and heavy with gold rings, beads, and more, "are the marks of a warrior who has earned honors in battle!" she declared.

Gabriel let a slow grin cut his face, then said, "Oh, I believe you. The way you threw that knife at me, even though you were lying flat of your back and about unconscious, showed you were a fighter!"

She relaxed and lowered her gaze, "I am glad I did not kill you."

Gabriel chuckled, "I am too! So, how 'bout you travelin' with us? We're headin' to Fort Carondelet, and since you know this country, you could keep us from getting lost."

She looked from Gabriel to Ezra and back. "I will go with you."

"Good, good. We'll rearrange the packs so you can ride, but you also need to know there are some men on our trail who want to kill us, so there will be some danger. That's why we're travelin' at night."

"Why do they want to kill you? Are you enemies?"

Gabriel paused a moment before answering, "That about covers it. Yeah, we are enemies."

"Ain't that the truth!" mumbled Ezra as he rose to bring the horses near.

Dusk hung heavy over the timber as the sun tucked itself away beyond the far treetops. With the dim light, they pushed out of the trees and gigged their horses forward to cross the placid waters of the Niangua River. A sandbar at the point of an island gave footing to the horses just past the half-way point, and then the sandbank of the far shore beckoned the four horses and their riders. All three stepped down, giving the horses free rein to shake off the excess water and grab a mouthful of green grass.

Honey Bear was very observant and asked Gabriel, "You have a quiver of arrows, but I do not see a bow?"

"It's there—that wide sheath beneath the left stirrup," said Gabriel, pointing to the wide fringed sheath. With the river water barely reaching the bellies of the horses, he had held the sheathed bow across his pommel to keep it dry but replaced it as soon as they were on the shore. She frowned, then looked at Gabriel, her expression showing her question.

He chuckled, "I know, it's different than what you're used to seeing. It's what is called a Mongol bow. It came from a war-like tribe far across the big water."

She had heard the black robes speak of the big water but had never traveled that far and was skeptical of their descriptions. But she nodded, showing her disbelief.

"When we camp, I'll show it to you. Let you shoot it if you can."

She scowled at Gabriel, breathed deep, and lifted her shoulders, "I can shoot any bow a man can."

Gabriel chuckled, "We'll see, we'll see."

When they first encountered the Pomme de Terre river, they were atop a steep bluff overlooking the stream some one hundred fifty feet below, but Honey Bear led them to a winding brushy draw that brought them to a wide meadow that dropped into the stream. They crossed the smaller river by the first light of day, wanting to make camp on the far shore that harbored good cover and grass for the animals.

"This is called the Pomme de Terre River, French for soil apple or potato. But we called it the Big Bone River for the bones of the big animals with long horns that were found here."

Gabriel looked at the woman, "Big animals with long horns?"

"Yes, they had long noses and horns beside their noses. Big ears, too, and they were bigger than the lodges of our people. But we only saw the drawings on the walls of the caves, for they were all gone by our lifetime."

The easy crossing was quickly made, and each one stretched, bent, and twisted to get the kinks out after the night's ride. Stripping the gear from the horses, Gabriel dropped the packs beneath a pair of large oaks that would be good shelter, and the long branches that still held tenaciously to the gold and brown leaves would filter the smoke from their fire. He gave the horses rubdowns with hands full of grass while Ezra gathered wood and started the fire. Although nothing had been said about responsibilities, Bear readily gathered the foodstuffs and sorted through what they had to begin her preparations. She chuckled when she found the cornmeal and was quick to set to work making cornmeal biscuits. Ezra had fetched the coffee pot full of water and set it by the now crackling fire.

"Before you get too involved, let me show you this bow," suggested Gabriel.

Honey Bear smiled and stood to come to his side. He was sitting on a large log that had shed its bark years ago and had probably been used by many others over the course of the decade it had lain at the edge of the clearing. The campsite had been used by others, probably Indians, or even French or Spanish explorers, and the remains of old fires were evident.

Gabriel pulled the bow from the leather case, and Bear frowned when she saw the unstrung weapon. The birchbark covering was tight to the bow and gave the impression the bow was constructed of the same bark, but Gabriel, seeing her expression, said, "No, that's just the covering to protect it. Under the cover, the bow is made of the horn of the big-horn ram, wood, and sinew. The string is made of rawhide from the hide of a horse." He handed the unstrung bow to her to examine and she carefully fingered it, turning it over and looking at each detail. She held it up, but the unstrung Mongol bow is the shape of a semi-circle and she held it with the open portion of the circle toward her.

Gabriel shook his head, took the bow, and said, "This way. But let me string it first." He sat down, put one foot on either side of the hand grip, and pulled on the limbs with both hands, carefully fingering the string toward the ends and the notches. Bear giggled as she watched Gabriel's contortions and facial expressions as he exerted the strength to string the weapon. Once strung, the bow showed its completely different shape, with the limbs curving away from the handle, back to the string, and away from the shooter.

He stood and nocked an arrow, and with the jade thumb ring, he made the fist and pulled back the string to bring the bow to a full draw, then let the arrow fly. It cleared the tops of the trees at the far edge of the clearing and arced down to embed itself in the grass in a far meadow about two hundred fifty yards distant. Honey Bear stood frozen, looking with shaded eyes at the far meadow, then turned to look at Gabriel. He grinned, then handed her the bow and an arrow. He showed her how to use her thumb with the thumb ring, locking her fingers over the thumb for the draw. He stepped back and let her nock the arrow, then try to draw the bow. She expected it to be no different than what she was used to, but the first effort barely moved the string. She looked wide-eyed at Gabriel, then back at the string. She lifted the bow again and tried to draw, but only succeeded in about a two-inch pull, then scowled, lowered the bow and removed the thumb ring. She lifted the bow again and tried it with her usual three-finger pull and had less success than before.

Ezra had been watching and said, "Don't feel bad. I can't shoot that thing either. He can only do it 'cuz he's been using it since he was a sprout and has developed the muscles needed."

She shook her head and said, "I do not understand. I have never seen anyone shoot an arrow that far." She nodded toward the far meadow, "and that bow. . ." but words failed her, and she shook her head and went to the fire while Gabriel went to the far meadow to retrieve the arrow. He had just stepped past a big ash tree when movement caught his eye. He nocked an arrow and sent the feathered missile into the chest of a young buck that was returning from his evening's water. He grinned, knowing they were cooking the last of their fresh meat for supper. This was a special bounty all would appreciate.

15 / Osage

As dusk dropped its curtain of darkness, the trio moved out. The three-quarter moon was waning, but clouds were moving in and showed the silver lining with the moon hiding behind. But the way was certain and known by Honey Bear as she followed the dim game trail that twisted through the trees. The chill in the air warned of a change in the weather and Gabriel looked often to the clouds, hoping to get in a good night's travel before the clouds dumped their cargo of white. The wind was picking up and the men lifted their collars and hunkered into their shirts, trying to forestall the cold without stopping. As they rocked in their saddles, Gabriel thought of the woman, then turned in his saddle to loosen the bedroll behind him and fumbled with a blanket. He retied the rest and gigged Ebony toward the woman. He held out the blanket, which she gladly received and wrapped it around her shoulders, lifting the edge over her head and holding it tightly at her neck. "We're gonna hafta find us some cover soon since that storm might cut loose anytime!" said Gabriel, stating the obvious, and received a nod in return.

He had no sooner spoken than the snow began, big fluffy flakes that drifted slowly to the ground and disappeared in the warm grasses. The wind had slackened and the moon escaped from behind the big cloud, bringing a mystical light that the snowflakes, dancing from side to side, rode to the ground. They were moving due north, bound for the Osage River, where they would turn west and follow the river's course to the site of Fort Carondelet, which sat at the confluence of the Little Osage and Marais des Cygnes Rivers. Now moving through the trees, the random flakes that made their way past the remaining leaves found rest on their shoulders and the manes of the horses. With the shuffling gait of the animals, the creak of the leather, and the bobbing of the horses' heads, the mesmerizing and soothing effect began to usher in the beginnings of slumber to the hypnotized riders. Honey Bear reined up and motioned for them to step down and give the horses a drink, and for the riders to stretch and partake of some of the freshly smoked meat she'd prepared overnight. She had gathered some late-season berries and pounded them together with the meat after smoking, making a sort of pemmican. Gabriel and Ezra had never tasted the native delicacy before and were surprised but pleased at its taste.

The snow continued to fall, and as the night cooled, the snow began to pile up. The horses kicked up puffs with each step, often twitching their ears to rid them of snow, and the riders, now with their heavy coats and blankets about them, peered from between upturned collars and pulled-down hats for an occasional glimpse of the trail. Gabriel took a quick look at their backtrail and saw their tracks were filling in almost as quickly as they passed. He was pleased it would be difficult for anyone to follow.

With white all about them and everything seen through the silver filter of the light of the moon, the path before them seemed illuminated, giving an otherworldly effect to their travel. Nothing moved aside from the trio of travelers, proving all the forest's animals had more wisdom than man to be out on a night such as this. The snow muffled any and all sounds of their movement, each flake adding to the depth and stillness of the night. They stayed close to one another, knowing how easy it would be, once separated, to be lost and perhaps never found. With the snow now past the hocks of the horses and threatening to deepen dramatically, Gabriel pushed up beside Honey Bear, "I think we need to find shelter 'fore it gets too deep to find firewood and such."

"Yes. I know of an overhang and cave not too far. It was made before the river changed its course and is big enough for us and the horses," answered Bear, not stopping. "We will be there soon."

"Good," and nodding heavenward, he said, "Those dark clouds are gonna cover the moon soon, and it'll be harder to see anything!" declared Gabriel, dropping back to follow Bear's broken trail. She nodded and turned back to watch the path before them.

It was late morning when Honey Bear reined up near a

tall bluff and dropped to the ground, the snow almost to her knees. She motioned to the bluff and Gabriel moved close, still astride Ebony, but the horse was being a little skittish, looking toward the dark maw under the overhang, nostrils flaring and ears forward. Gabriel glanced at the woman, "Something's wrong; he doesn't like what he's smelling. Could be just some varmint, or maybe a bear."

"There have been bears here before. Maybe he's smelling their bedding or scat or something else. There might be nothing but the smell that's bothering him," suggested Honey Bear.

Gabriel stepped down to join Bear and Ezra but had slipped his Ferguson from the scabbard. He looked around for something to use as a torch, saw a nearby white pine, and kicked around beneath it for a couple of big cones. Ezra had broken off some dead twigs and small branches and kicked away the drifted snow beneath the tree, and quickly got a small fire going. Gabriel had prepared his torch, stuck an additional cone inside his jacket, chose to carry one of the saddle pistols, and eared back the hammer for one barrel. He passed his Ferguson to Honey Bear, "You know how to use this?" he asked. Then seeing a question on her face, he demonstrated. "Cock the hammer with your finger on this trigger. That sets this trigger," he pointed to the smaller rear trigger, "and this one makes it shoot! Just make sure I ain't in the way!" He looked at both Ezra and Honey Bear, "I'm just checkin' to make sure there's nothing in there. If there is, I'll do my best to sneak out without disturbing anything.

But I might have to shoot my way out, so if I come running, be ready!"

Ezra chuckled, "Oh, we'll be ready all right. Might be up a tree, but we'll be ready!"

He put the cone of the torch in the flame, saw it flare, and started into the cave. The torch sputtered a bit, but he was soon under the overhang, and shadows danced on the wall. He pointed his way with the torch, and purposefully moved into the black mouth. He was quiet with his steps, watching his footing and any loose gravel or rocks near his feet. A stream no more than two hands-breadths wide giggled its way along one wall, finding its way out into the open and into the creek beyond. His nostrils were filled with the bitter stench of bear, but he had to be certain there were none inside and he continued. Stepping carefully and looking as far as the torchlight allowed, he watched for movements that would be hard to make out with the shadows from the torch.

He had gone about twenty yards into the cave when he froze, believing he'd heard a huffing sound like that of a bear. He waved the torch back and forth, trying to look beyond the bright flame and make out any movement. The roar of an angry bear filled the entire cavern and reverberated off the walls. The sound made every nerve in Gabriel stand on edge, and his eyes widened to see the entire maw of the cave filled with the black of the beast before him. Another roar and the flame of the torch sputtered much like Gabriel's nerves, but when the now-upright bear took a lumbering step toward him, his two massive forelegs stretched out and long claws showing at the ends, Gabriel brought the .54 caliber pistol up and pulled the trigger.

The blast of the pistol bounced off the walls, sounding like three or four shots, and the lead ball penetrated the thick black fur, showing a puff of dust and bringing a grunt from the bear. But he roared again, coming closer, jaws snapping, grunting and growling, and Gabriel, backstepping away, fired the second barrel. The flash of fire, the cloud of thick smelling smoke and the impact of the bullet dropped the bear to all fours. But still he came, and Gabriel threw the torch at the beast, turned tail, and ran for the opening. When he burst out, he shouted, "It's coming!" and dove into the deep snow face-first.

Ezra fired first, his bullet scoring a hit that took the bear between his head and shoulder, plowing through the muscle into the body cavity and causing the bear to stumble and fall on his chin. But he quickly rose, looking for his attacker. Then the Ferguson in the hands of Honey Bear roared its challenge to the beast, sending the big lead ball to plow its furrow just under the bear's chin into his chest. The bear choked, trying to growl, then stumbled and fell, unmoving in the snow. The silence was broken only by the snorting and blowing of the horses, unhappy with being tethered in the trees within smelling distance of the bear. Ezra walked slowly toward the downed bear, pistol in hand, and poked it with his foot, and again, and there was no movement or sound from the black beast. Ezra stood tall, looked to his friend who had risen from his snowy grave, and then to

Honey Bear, still holding the Ferguson at her side, and said, "Show's over, folks!"

Honey Bear laughed, Gabriel chuckled, and they came together by the big carcass. Honey Bear said, "He's fat, good for grease. Meat too!"

Gabriel chuckled, "I like the looks of that hide. Won't that make a warm coat?"

"First, we need to get him outta the way, get a fire goin' in the cave to get rid of the stink so the horses'll go in there, and make us a warm camp," suggested Ezra.

At Bear's direction, they dragged the carcass under the far end of the overhang, and she took over the skinning and dressing while they tended to the cave, fire, and camp. It took a while for the skittish horses to go into the cave, but between the smoke of the fire and the presence of the men, they soon settled down, and the men rubbed them down, piling grass gathered from under the bigger trees before them. Ezra was tasked with cooking while Gabriel gathered the wood and tended to the packs and other gear. When the meal was ready, Honey Bear returned, carrying a bundled packet of bear fat she would render into grease. She walked wide of the horses as they watched her, wide-eyed and leery of the bear smell, but she spoke to them as she passed, and they soon settled down.

The snow continued to pile up, and by the end of the day, it was knee-deep. With the heavy cloud cover and the waning moon, traveling would be too dangerous to risk. It would be too easy for a horse to misstep and break a leg, and the same weather that prevented their travel would also hinder any followers. They gathered more firewood and grass for the horses and decided to have a rest, but Honey Bear was determined to render the bear fat and smoke most of the meat, so she stayed busy, and often recruited the men to help. In their idle time, Bear started teaching the men the universal sign language used by most of the Plains Indians. Both Ezra and Gabriel were learning and appreciated the work of the woman, knowing the smoked meat and grease would benefit them greatly, but the sign language might be the most useful.

16 / Village

The maw of the cavern faced the rising sun, and the golden orb easily filled the dark cave with its lances of pink and gold. The trio had spent much of the night tending the smoking meat and practicing their sign language, and the brightness of morning caught them still in their blankets. Bear was the first to the smoldering embers that lay beneath the meat racks, and, using the coals, she started a cookfire for their morning fare. Ezra went to the mouth of the cave, stood and stretched with the sun full in his face. He took a moment to bask in the warmth of the sun, admiring the white-blanketed valley, trees humbled beneath the weight of the snow, the colors of the sky painted by the rising sun, and the promise of a clear sky for the day.

Gabriel sat beside the fire, waiting for the water in the coffeepot to tell him it was ready for the fresh grounds and thinking about the coming day. He looked up as Ezra approached, "I don't see any reason for us to wait till dark to move out. A blind man could follow our trail from here, even in the dark!"

"Are we even sure they're still followin' us?" asked Ezra.

Chuckling, Gabriel answered, "The only way we can be sure is to let them catch up with us. Then we can go ask 'em if they're after us. 'Course, if they say no, then I guess we'll be all right, but if they say yes, I think we'd be in a bit of a predicament, wouldn't you say?"

Ezra cocked his head and scowled, "Has anybody ever used words like condescending, arrogant, skeptical, supercilious, cocky, and other such terms when they describe you?"

"All too often, my friend, all too often. But of course, you and I know the truth of the matter, don't we?" remarked Gabriel, grinning.

"Humph. I'm beginning to think that is the truth!"

Gabriel laughed, poured two cups of coffee, handed one to Ezra, and added, "Surely, you're not serious, are you?"

Both men laughed now, and Ezra turned to Bear, "Think we can make the fort sometime today?"

"I hope to find the village of my people before we go to the fort. The leaders talked about making their winter camp nearby, but this is the first winter for the fort, and my people are, how to say, careful." She had some johnnycake cooking in the pan at the edge of the fire and flipped it as she spoke. She lifted her eyes to Gabriel, "I think my people would welcome you."

"Then I guess we better pack up and get a move on. What say?" said Gabriel, looking at Ezra for his response. After a grin and a nod from his friend, they finished their coffee, grabbed a hot johnnycake and a couple pieces of pemmican, and got busy.

Bear yielded the lead to Gabriel after her horse stumbled in the deep snow. She had been breaking trail for most of the morning and was tiring quickly. When she signaled Gabriel to take the lead, she stepped down, the unbroken snow at least knee-deep kept her in front of her horse and stepping in the tracks of the big black. She soon tired and swung back aboard the sorrel, finding her seat on the blanket that covered the packsaddle. It wasn't the most comfortable, but it was better than walking, and once she pushed back against the soft-sided packs, she had a modicum of comfort. She was no sooner settled in her seat than Gabriel reined up, holding up his hand to stop the others.

Still back in the trees, Gabriel leaned forward along Ebony's neck, peering through the half-naked branches at a party of Indians, all warriors, that had come from the river and were moving silently through the deep snow, evidently on either a hunting expedition or a raid. Bear had stepped down and now stood beside the big black, looking at the warriors. She turned to Gabriel, "Those are Pawnee. It is a war party, and they are searching for my village." She spoke softly, but the alarm was evident in her voice and manner.

"They are enemies of my people. They come at this time and in the time of greening to raid our villages and take captives. They have a ceremony called the Morning Star ritual where they sacrifice young women captives, so they have good soil and good crops," explained Bear.

"It was the Pawnee that took you captive, wasn't it?" asked Gabriel.

"Yes. Those are from the same band. That was Knife Chief leading them. He has been their chief for many seasons, but his people are not happy. The ritual is his way of making his people follow him."

"When you say sacrifice, do you mean he has a ritual where he actually kills the woman?" asked Ezra, frowning.

"Yes. She is shot with many arrows, the shaman cuts her chest so she will bleed, and the men hold her above the soil so her blood covers much of the land."

"That's barbaric!" declared Ezra, "I mean, sacrifice? We can't let that happen!"

"Now who's getting us into trouble?" asked Gabriel, grinning, but both men knew they were in agreement about doing what they could to stop the raid. Gabriel looked at Bear, "Do you think we can get to your village before they do?"

She thought for a moment, then looked back to Gabriel, "I do not know for sure where the village is this season. I believe it will be near the fort, but it could be anywhere."

Gabriel looked at the line of warriors that moved into the trees, quickly counting and thinking. "They've got over twenty warriors and the element of surprise. But, so do we, have the surprise element, I mean. But first, tell me, Bear, when they attack a village, how do they do it?"

Bear briefly explained, "They make a distraction, then attack the other end of the village. One or more warriors take the captives while the others fight. Then they turn and run."

"That's what I figured. Now, here's what I'm thinking..." He explained his tactics for the coming fight. "Bear, you've already proven you know how to shoot, so I'm gonna let you have one of the double-barreled saddle pistols and one of the extra rifles my Pa insisted I bring. Ezra, you take the other extra rifle, your two pistols, and your rifle. And with what I've got, I think we can convince them of the error of their ways. Agreed?"

Both Ezra and Honey Bear nodded their agreement as they stepped back aboard their horses. Gabriel led the way as they began to follow the Pawnee, taking advantage of the broken trail through the deep snow. He would often lean down on Ebony's neck to watch the trail ahead, ensuring they weren't too close and give themselves away.

It was a challenge to stay close behind the party and not be discovered. The low rolling hills, most covered with now-naked trees, did little to prevent their being seen. With each rise, Gabriel had to move to the crest on foot, carefully scan the way before them, and search the terrain for any scouts who might have been left behind to watch the backtrail. Occasionally they had to stay in the thicker timber, avoiding the open meadows, and break their own trail, tiring the horses.

They neared another crest, and Gabriel stepped down to make his way to the top. As he neared the edge, he dropped to his knees, looking over the knob to see the Pawnee stopped at the edge of the trees on the far side of a small meadow. They had dismounted and were gathered together in the trees, apparently giving their horses a brief rest before the attack. He looked beyond and saw the thin traces of smoke spiraling upward in the clear air of the lowlands. He turned and motioned the others to come to his side, then pointed out the smoke to Bear, "I think that might be your village."

She nodded her agreement, then looked at the Pawnee, "Yes," she said, pointing to the warriors below with her chin, "and they will attack soon!"

"Do you think you could go through that draw yonder and make it to the village to warn them?" asked Gabriel, pointing out the dip in the terrain that would give her cover but also had unbroken snow.

Bear looked at the lay of the land, calculating her route, and said, "I will go," and started back to the horses. Gabriel stripped the horse of the extra packs and other gear and told Bear, "Ezra and I will do as we planned, so make sure your people know we're on your side," grinning as he spoke.

He handed her the saddle pistol and gave her a quick lesson on the weapon, then strung a powder horn and a possibles bag over her shoulders, handed up the extra rifle, and said, "We'll see you soon!"

She lifted her head, looking from Gabriel to Ezra and back again, "Yes!" she answered, then put her heels to the sorrel and went into the trees.

Gabriel looked at Ezra, "Looks like we've got our work cut out for us, my friend." He bent to pick up the extra gear and started to the chestnut gelding packhorse, followed by Ezra with a soft-sided pannier in his hands, and he said, "We'll need to put some of this on our horses since it's more'n what one packhorse can handle."

"Uuumhmm," answered Gabriel, doing as suggested. Once the gear was secured, he walked back to the crest to see what the Pawnee were up to and quickly slid back down. He stood and started for Ebony as he said over his shoulder, "They're movin' out. I think the attack's about to start."

"Then we better give chase!" declared Ezra as he swung aboard his bay.

When they crested the hill, the last of the war party had moved into the trees and was rounding the point of the knob that separated them from the village. The thick trees, although denuded by the snow and cold, still gave cover to the band. They were about three hundred yards from the edge of the village, and Gabriel saw two warriors move out from the band, which had stopped in the trees.

Gabriel turned and whispered to Ezra, "They're gonna be the distraction. I think the horse herd is on the far side of the village. That's probably what they're gonna do—make 'em think the raiders are after horses."

Ezra sat his horse beside Gabriel and Ebony, they were on a slight slope behind the war party. As they watched, they were choosing their shooting positions for when they followed the attackers toward the village. They slipped their rifles from the scabbards, laid them across the pommels, and checked the loads. After a quick check of their pistols, they were ready. But Gabriel saw they had a moment, so he pulled the Mongol bow from its sheath and awkwardly strung it, his first attempt at doing it on horseback. Ezra laughed, "It's a good thing you don't have to do that when somebody's chargin'. You'd be dead in a hurry!"

17 / Pawnee

The war party was focused on the wide break in the trees that offered entry into the winter camp of the Osage. A slight rise on the left of a broad tree-covered knob overlooked the many bark lodges, the stream at the west edge, and the central grounds. Between the Osage River and the camp of the people, the trees were thick, although mostly bare of leaves.

Gabriel and Ezra were less than fifty yards behind the war party when Gabriel had a sudden idea. Leaning over to Ezra, he whispered, "While they wait for the diversion, I'm gonna take off through those trees and see if I can create a distraction of my own." He pointed to their left, "You work your way through those trees, and maybe we can hit 'em before they do too much damage!"

Without waiting for a response, Gabriel shoved his rifle back in the scabbard, brought his quiver to his pommel, hanging it from the saddle horn, and nocked an arrow, then dug his heels into Ebony's sides and took off through the trees. Ezra, stunned at his friend's quick change of plans, watched him for just a second, then reined his big bay into the trees to flank the war party.

The usual thunder of hooves was muted by the deep snow and the carpet of leaves underneath. Gabriel lay low on Ebony's neck, twisting and winding through the trees, glancing to the side to get a fix on the war party. He knew they would soon start their charge, and he wanted to be near their right flank. He remembered the illustrations of the Mongol warriors of their charges into battle, using the powerful bow and shooting from astride a running horse. He had all the confidence in Ebony, but he wasn't certain about his own competence, having never tried shooting from horseback, much less a running horse. He also acknowledged that man is not always in control of his circumstances.

His course had brought him parallel with the Pawnee, and a quick glance through the trees showed they were on the move. Using his knees, he guided Ebony closer to the war party, and as they screamed their war cries and kicked their horses to a run for their charge, he moved into the clear less than twenty yards on their flank. He rose up, drew the bow to full draw, and sent his first arrow on its flight. He quickly nocked another, drew back, and let it fly. He saw both arrows take their mark, the first one unseating the warrior, the second burying itself in the side of a warrior who slumped forward, tangling his hands in the mane of his horse.

They were upon the village, screaming and shouting war cries that added to the din of gunshots and the screams of women and children. Ebony swerved to miss a lodge, almost unseating Gabriel, but he grabbed mane, righted himself, and found another target. He quickly released the arrow, then grabbed the rein to pull Ebony to a stop. He hung the bow on the horn dropped to his feet, rifle in hand, then eared back the hammer as he took a knee and followed the mounted Pawnee with his sights. He squeezed off his shot and quickly lowered the rifle, spun the trigger guard, opened the breech, and reloaded. He closed the breech, watching for his target, put the powder in the frizzen pan, and swiftly fired again, sending another Pawnee to the Great Beyond.

Catching movement out of his peripheral vision, he snatched the saddle pistol and turned as an arrow whispered past his head. He snapped off a shot that caught the charging warrior full in the chest and the .54 caliber ball tore a massive hole in the man's back, having struck the spine. The warrior slid off the running horse to tumble into the snow no more than two yards from the feet of Gabriel. He searched for another target, but they had gone deeper into the village. He swung back aboard Ebony, took the time to reload both rifle and pistol, and then started toward the melee.

Two of the many lodges were aflame after the charging Pawnee kicked the cookfires toward the structures. The smoke from the fires and the rifles lay low among the lodges, and women were screaming and grabbing their children, trying to find cover in or near the bark-covered frames. Gabriel picked his way through the village, searching for a target. The Pawnee, with their thick hair in braids decorated with feathers, were easily distinguished from the Osage, who plucked the hair from their faces and heads, leaving only a roach at the back. He heard a scream and turned to see a Pawnee dragging a young woman, kicking her and grabbing her hair, as she tried to free herself. With a fluid movement, Gabriel swung his Ferguson toward the man, firing from his side and sending the monstrous.65 caliber ball through the man's chest, dropping him to his face. The girl rose, looked at Gabriel, and ran behind the nearest lodge.

Honey Bear rode into the village at a run, shouting the warning of the coming Pawnee. She slid to the ground, rifle in hand, and hollered to the small cluster of warriors who had risen to watch her ride into the midst of the village. She shouted, "Pawnee! There!" pointing back to the break in the trees that was the entry to the village. "They're going to try for the herd, but that's a diversion. The attack will come from there! A white man and a black man will attack the Pawnees. They are *friends!*"

The warriors scattered, going to their lodges for their weapons. Women grabbed children to retreat to the lodges. Two of the elders went quickly to Honey Bear, one recognizing her, and began asking questions about the attackers. They barked commands to several of the Osage warriors who had returned with their weapons, and a quickly organized defense was mounted. Bear took up position beside one of the lodges, dropping to one knee and bringing the rifle up. The sudden outburst of war cries and screams of the raiders startled her, but her resolve steadied her aim. At the head of the Pawnee, one man, face painted in crimson and black, feathers flopping in the wind, mounted on a roan horse, locked eyes with Bear and charged directly toward her. Bear breathed deep, narrowed her aim, and squeezed off the shot. The hammer dropped and flint slid down the frizzen, dropping sparks into the pan and shooting smoke to the side. Then the big rifle roared, spitting smoke and death, the ball taking the charging leader just under the chin and through the throat, jerking his head back and silencing his scream as he tumbled off the back of his horse.

Bear leaned back against the lodge and let the horse race past, then brought up the double-barreled saddle pistol to pick another target. The mass of raiders was jumbled together and she fired into their midst. The roar and smoke of the pistol caught the attention of an attacker as the bullet blossomed red on the chest of another. The first attacker, certain Bear had fired her only shot, swerved his horse toward her, raised his lance, and readied his throw, but the second barrel boomed and the big ball carried its message of death through the bone breastplate and into the chest of the Pawnee. His eyes flared and his strength faded as he dropped his lance and looked at his chest to see the shattered bloody breastplate, and his head slumped as he tumbled to the side, falling in a heap that was trampled by the horses of his warriors behind him.

Bear stepped behind the lodge and busied herself reloading her weapons. The screams and cries of both attackers and attacked filled the air, sending lances of fear into her heart as she fumbled with the balls, patches, and powder. Suddenly

a big black horse was beside her and she looked up to see
Gabriel, who asked, "You doin' all right?"

She looked at him, then down at her feeble efforts at reloading, and said, "Yes!" The question brought added resolve
as she looked at her friend. He said, "Here, let me reload that
pistol for you," and reached down for the double-barreled
weapon. He deftly reloaded, primed the pans, and said,
"They'll be coming back through." He pointed with his chin,
"You stay here, and I'll go see if I can hurry 'em along."

Ezra had easily worked through the trees and dropped to the
ground, then tethered his bay to a tree and trotted to a patch
of cover that held some boulders and brush. He mounted
one of the smaller boulders that nestled behind a larger one,
then, grinning, he scanned his area, checked his weapons,
and readied himself. Within only seconds to spare, he heard
the charge begin and lifted his rifle for his first shot. A big
warrior astraddle a sizeable dapple grey was his nearest target, and he readily brought his sights to bear, squeezed off his
shot, and unseated the big man. But as he laid down his rifle,
reaching for the second, he saw the big warrior rise and look
his direction.

Ezra lifted the spare rifle to take aim at the standing
Pawnee, he brought the front blade sight between the
buckhorns of the rear sight, breathed deep, let some out,
and squeezed off his shot. The rifle boomed and blossomed
smoke, obscuring Ezra's view of the target, but the big man
parted the cloud as he charged toward Ezra. He grabbed

his saddle pistol, cocking it as he brought it up and quickly pulled the trigger. The pistol bucked in his hand and the ball found its way to pierce the charging warrior's chest, but he didn't slow, only screamed and raised his lance as he charged. Without taking his eyes off the Pawnee, Ezra snatched his belt pistol up, cocked it, and fired. Again, he saw the blossom of blood at the man's chest, but he only stuttered a step and kept coming. Ezra growled, grabbing for the big ironwood Potawatomie war club hanging at his back, and brought it around as he stood watching the big warrior come. He lifted the club above his head, snarled out a growl, and brought it down, the blade taking the warrior at the base of his neck at his shoulder. The big man dropped to his knees and tried to bring up his lance, then fell on his face at Ezra's feet.

Ezra stepped back, almost falling, to be seated on the boulder, then his attention turned to the charging horde of Pawnee. Most of them had passed him by, but one warrior had seen the attack by his companion and reined his horse around to face Ezra. He lifted his lance, leaned forward, and kicked his horse into a running charge. The only weapon left for Ezra was his war club and he hopped off the boulder and raised it shoulder-high, awaiting the charging Pawnee. The screaming warrior laid low on his horse's neck and watched as Ezra danced back and forth on the balls of his feet, waiting. The Pawnee rose up, lifting his lance for a throw, and launched the long weapon in a low arc toward his enemy. Ezra stepped lightly to the side, letting the lance barely miss his shoulder, then jumped in the air, startling the horse and making him swerve as he brought down the big war club on the head of the Pawnee. He heard the crack as the man's skull was bashed in, and the warrior plummeted from his mount, bouncing end over end in the grass.

Ezra looked around for any other threats, bounded to his boulder where the weapons lay, and began reloading. He mounted the bay and started for the edge of the village, knowing if any of the Pawnee survived, they would return on this path. He saw a likely spot, tethered the bay to a pole beside a lodge, and took his position to await their return.

Suddenly, two mounted warriors came thundering toward him, but he saw that both men had women captives laying over the withers of their horses, and the warriors were leaning forward, putting part of their weight on the women so they could not escape. They came at a full gallop and Ezra brought up his rifle, looking for a target, but the warriors were using the women as shields and he couldn't fire without hitting the captives. They rumbled past, looking only at their escape route, and Ezra saw both women were actually young girls, fighting and kicking, to no avail.

He looked toward the rest of the village, seeing nothing but smoke and dust, but the cacophony of a battle that still raged gave no illusion it was abating. He looked toward the fleeing men and their captives and made his decision. He swung aboard his bay, but instead of pursuing the warriors, he charged into the village, searching for Gabriel.

18 / Chase

"Gabriel!" shouted Ezra, seeing his friend come from behind a bark lodge. Gabriel reined Ebony in at Ezra's side, "What? Are you all right?" he asked, looking toward the fight, which seemed to be abating.

"They've got two girls captive, and they've taken to the trees!" he shouted, pointing back toward the camp's entry.

"How many Pawnee?"

"Two, or at least, that's all I saw," answered Ezra, reining around to start their pursuit.

"Let's get Honey Bear. She knows this country and the Pawnee!" suggested Gabriel.

Within moments the trio was in pursuit, Bear leading as she leaned over the horse's neck, looking at the tracks. With so many from the attack and the usual coming and going, it was difficult but not impossible for the experienced warrior woman to follow the trail of the fleeing captors. Often rising up to look at the trail ahead, she turned to Gabriel, "They're going back the same way. Maybe we can cut them off at the river crossing." Without waiting for an answer, she turned her mount into the trees, taking an angular trail toward the Osage River.

The naked branches whipped at them and the remaining snow that still clung to the trees dropped on their shoulders, and the horses wove in and out of the thick timber. Before them, they heard the splashing of water and knew the captors were crossing the river. Bear pushed on, and as they came to the riverbank, she urged her sorrel over the edge and into the frigid water, breaking the thin ice at the river's edge. The horses hunched and fought the current, but the river was low, and the muddy footing hindered them. Just downstream, they saw the two Pawnee and their captives climb the far bank, aiming for the trees and their escape.

The three horses splashed and pushed through the current, digging at the muddy bottom with their hooves, urged on by their riders. Once on the sandbar bank, they rose from the water and charged into the trees. Just beyond the trees that lined the river, a wide basin of meadow showed as a white blanket across the flats. The two Pawnee had slowed to a trot, following the broken trail made when the war party came through that morning. One of the warriors twisted around in his seat just as the trio of pursuers broke from the trees. He shouted the warning to his friend and both men kicked their tired horses into a gallop, seeking to escape their pursuers.

Gabriel and Bear saw them at the same time, and Gabriel

dug his heels into Ebony's ribs. The stallion lunged forward and stretched out as he broke into a run. Gabriel lay along his neck, encouraging his friend, who loved to run. It had been some time since the two had let it all loose and ran, and Ebony responded to the urging of his rider, his eyes on the two horses ahead. Never one to let any other horse best him, the big black stallion stretched his neck, nose in the wind, and his long legs flew over the ground, snow splattering with every footfall.

Behind the black came Bear on her sorrel and Ezra on his bay. Although the big black was lengthening his lead, they fought for every foot of ground, determined to stay in the race until the end. Ebony gained on the fleeing Pawnee, who twisted around to see how close their pursuers were, and with each sighting, they kicked their horses harder, bound and determined to escape with their prizes. But neither Ebony nor Gabriel was willing to let that happen, and the stallion seemed to catch fresh wind and dug deeper.

Within moments, the Andalusian stallion, with mane flowing in the air and tail pointing behind him, was pulling alongside the steel dust grey of the Pawnee. As they neared, Gabriel drew his tomahawk from his belt, and reared back. The black leaned into the Indian pony, causing the rider to grab for the mane, but the 'hawk in the hand of Gabriel slashed down on the warrior's shoulder, cutting through to the bone, and the crunch was audible as the warrior screamed his agony. With no use of his now-broken arm, the Pawnee released the mane, and the second blow from Gabriel scraped his skull, laying the bone bare and peeling off his ear, and the warrior slid to the side, grabbing at his captive as he fell.

Gabriel jammed the 'hawk's handle into his belt, reached for the tunic of the woman, who rode belly-down across the horse's withers, and dragged her across the neck of Ebony as he began to slow his friend to a walk. He saw the shadowy images of Ezra and Bear as they continued the chase after the second Pawnee. As Gabriel reined to a stop, he released the wiggling and struggling girl, letting her drop to the ground. She fell on her back, scrambled to her feet, and turned to look at Gabriel. Her eyes were wide, and fear showed as she breathed heavily and backed away from the white man on the big black horse. He spoke softly, using his limited knowledge of the Algonquian language, saying simply, "Friend," as he pointed at himself.

Ezra's bay had stretched out and was gaining on the Pawnee's dun-colored horse. As he drew nearer, his bay was matching the dun stride for stride, and Ezra reached to his back for his war club. With just a couple more strides, he believed he was close enough. With the girl lying across the withers, the Pawnee was leaning well forward, urging his tired mount on but still offered a tempting target to Ezra. He lifted the club shoulder-high, his right arm across his chest, and then, with a roundhouse swing, he brought the halberd blade across the space between them and took off the back of the man's head, sending him tumbling to the ground before the horse missed a step. Bear pulled alongside the Pawnee's horse, grabbing at the reins and the captive, and pulled the animal to a stop. The girl, still belly-down, looked around and, seeing the strange black man, tried to scramble off the horse to escape but was stopped by the words of Honey Bear, who spoke in the Osage dialect of the Algonquian language, "Wait, we are friends!"

The captive girl twisted around to see Bear and took a deep breath, obviously greatly relieved. She spoke to Bear, "You are Honey Bear! You brought the warning!"

"Yes, I am of your village. I was taken captive in the time of greening, but I escaped. These men," pointing to Ezra and back to Gabriel, "are my friends."

Ezra had caught the Pawnee's dun and led him back for the girl to ride. He went after the grey of the other captor and led it back to where Gabriel and the first girl waited. With Bear explaining, the girls expressed their thanks to the men and Bear as they mounted up to return to the village.

Gabriel led the way, choosing a path away from the trail of the war party. His concern was that there might be some survivors who would return the way they came, and he had shed enough blood for one day. As they entered the line of trees, they caught sight of six riders, Pawnee, about three hundred yards away and coming from the trees to follow their previous route. With neither group acknowledging the other, Gabriel continued into the trees to the bank of the Osage. They crossed just upstream of their previous journey, where a wider gravelly sandbar made the crossing less challenging.

As they rode into the village, they saw several people

tending to the burnt lodges that still smoldered and others taking care of the wounded. They would find out that only two had been killed, but four were wounded, while the Pawnee suffered the loss of fifteen killed. Gabriel and Ezra paid little attention to those who were carrying off the dead invaders but followed the lead of Bear as she led them and the captives to the central compound where the leaders waited.

Both men were somewhat spellbound at the sight of the Osage warriors. The stoic figures were impressive for their size, all over six feet tall and several close to seven feet. They had ear lobes that were cut open and carried many decorations. Tattoos of dark designs and figures were seen on many, and all had the bald dome that held the roach of hair at the back. They were a handsome tribe, and their visages were very intimidating as they glared at the visitors that rode into their midst.

Bear stepped down, motioning to Ezra and Gabriel to do the same. She stood before the group of three men who were obviously the leaders of the village and spoke to them, then turned to Gabriel and Ezra, gesturing to the leaders, "This is Blue Corn, our chief, and this man," pointing to the man to the left of the chief, "is Standing Elk, our shaman."

The leaders stepped forward and offered their hands to the visitors. Both men clasped hands with them and listened as the chief spoke, translated by Bear.

"We are grateful for your warning and your part of the battle. Our warriors speak highly of you and what you have done for our people. We are told you killed many of our enemies, and now Honey Bear tells of your rescue of the captives. We ask you to stay in our village and let our people show you their thanks."

Gabriel started to make excuses to leave, but the stern look from Bear changed his mind. He said, "We would be honored to stay, Chief."

"This is good. Honey Bear will show you to your lodge. We will feast this night," said Blue Corn, turning back to his lodge and dismissing the visitors.

Bear looked at her friends, smiling, and motioned for them to follow as she led them to a lodge for their stay. They were surprised to see their horses, including the chestnut packhorse, tethered near the lodge, and when Gabriel looked at Bear, she said, "I sent one of our young men back for the horse and packs before we left after the captives."

"You were all-fired sure that we would get them back. What if we'd failed?"

"You do not fail. I know you," she answered, grinning.

19 / Carondelet

They rode away from the village on a trail that took them to the bank of the Osage River and would lead to the new Fort Carondelet. Bear had chosen to go with the two friends to visit the fort and do some trading. She would need some new supplies for the winter's stay and to outfit her lodge, the one used by Gabriel and Ezra after the night's festivities at the central compound. The dancing and feasting were unlike anything ever seen by either Gabriel or Ezra, but it was an exciting time and a definite learning experience. As they left the village, the men were surprised to see two lines of poles on either side of the trail topped by the severed heads of the Pawnee warriors who had attacked the village.

Gabriel frowned, showing a face of disgust, reined up and looked at Bear, "What is that all about?" pointing to the gruesome figures atop the poles. Blood had trickled down the shafts, and the long hair of the warriors hung in matted strings. Most had the eyes gouged out and feces or other items stuffed in the mouths.

Bear, now riding a pony from the village herd, gigged her mount forward and urged the men to follow her quickly. As they rode from the macabre sight, she began to explain. "My people, the Ni-u-ko'n-ska, are known as fierce warriors. It is good for others to think that way since it saves much war. Other tribes take the scalps of their enemies, but our people do not. We put the heads of those who attack us on the poles outside the village to put fear in the hearts of others who would attack our people. When we wage war, we paint our bodies black, like Ezra, to make us more fearful, and when we attack a people, we kill them all, taking no captives. Then the heads are cut off and left, so other tribes will fear our people. We also do what the whites call "bluff" war, then we paint with other colors and black. We count coup and more but do not kill all. Many times, we take captives and sell them or take them into our families."

"That sounds a mite ghastly," declared Ezra, "but I guess it would make others afraid, all right."

"Our people do not like to kill others. When we do what you call ghastly, and it puts fear in those who would attack us so they do not go to war with us, we have saved many lives," added Bear as they broke from the trees at the edge of the river. Gabriel and Ezra were somewhat contemplative as they considered what they had learned of the Osage.

"Was that dance last night a celebration of your victory?" asked Gabriel, remembering the many dancers and the way the groups had interacted.

Bear smiled, "No, that was the story of our people's beginning, what you would call the creation story. You see, my people believe that Wah-kon-tah, the great mystery spirit, brought the people of the sky, Tzi-Sho, and the people of the land, Hun-Kah, together to form one people, the Ni-u-ska-ko'n-ska, or the Children of the Middle Waters. What the dancers did was to tell that story in dance."

Gabriel had taken the lead and now reined up as they saw the structure of Fort Carondelet standing as a sentinel near the confluence of the Little Osage and the Marais des Cygnes rivers. Gabriel's first impression was of two blocks stacked atop one another. The bottom square was of stone and was about ten yards square, perhaps a little more, with narrow vertical slits for light and as firing slots. Heavy plank doors that stood wide open marked the entry as well fortified but spacious, wide enough to accommodate bundles of furs and more. Sitting atop the square of stone, which stood at least ten feet tall, was another of heavy square logs that probably measured about nine feet tall. But the second story was set askew or diagonally, so the corners of the top story hung over the sides of the bottom story. It too had shooting slots, but those formed a cross and offered the shooter better visibility and shooting position. Several workers were busy atop the structure laying shake shingles in row after row. Several wagons, some still loaded, were assembled behind the structure, and a herd of mules was picketed near the trees.

Standing at the bottom and looking at the workers was a man, eyes shaded with one hand and the other stuck in his waistband. He was no doubt the supervisor of the construction. As Gabriel and company neared, the man turned to look at the new arrivals and grinned and walked toward them. "Hello! Hello! And welcome to Fort Carondelet!" The speaker had a receding hairline and thin dark wavy hair. Prominent eyebrows shadowed his dark eyes, but his smile was welcoming and appeared sincere. "Step down, please." He stepped forward, hand outstretched, "I'm Auguste Chouteau, and you're . . ."

Gabriel stepped down, smiling, and extended his hand, "I'm Gabe, and this," turning to his friends, "is Ezra and Honey Bear."

Chouteau grinned, shook hands with each one, but paused at Bear and asked, "You are Osage, aren't you?"

"Yes," she responded stoically.

Chouteau turned back to Gabriel, "As you can see, we're still building. I was told the post was finished, but when we arrived with the wagons, well, you can see what remains. However," and he rubbed his hands together, "we have plenty of goods if you're here to do some trading."

Gabriel grinned as he shook his head, "We've not much to trade, but we do need supplies, and we will pay."

"Fine, fine. We've offloaded three of the five wagons, and I have men sorting and stacking as we speak. But, if you'd like, we have coffee at the fire yonder, and I'd be pleased if you'd join me in a cup," suggested Chouteau, starting toward the fire that had died to embers and a thin trail of smoke.

It was unusual to sit at a table with chairs in the wilderness, but those were the first items unloaded, and to keep them out of the way of the men who were unpacking and stacking in the building, they were set beside the fire for convenience. The four sat and enjoyed the coffee as Chouteau told them of his plans for the post and more. "Once we get this underway, we'll start another one on the Verdigris River, further west."

"Just like this one?" asked Ezra, nodding toward the towering structure.

"Exactly," he declared, showing pride in his accomplishment. "If you notice, the way the top story is set diagonally, that's so the defenders can shoot through the holes in the floor planking at any attacker trying to get in the lower floor."

"Well, couldn't the attacker just shoot through the floor?" asked Ezra.

"Not through those planks. They're at least three inches thick and of hardwood. No sir."

"Will you still be trading with the Osage at your other post?" asked Gabriel.

"Yes, although the Kiowa are not but about two or three days from the Verdigris, they are not friendly the Osage. So, mostly, we'll be trading with them."

"Have you had any trouble here?" asked Ezra.

"No, no. These are good people, and we've traded with them for a few years now. We had a post further east on the Osage, nearer the Missouri, but this will replace that one."

"My people traveled to that post to trade in the time of greening," interjected Bear, nodding to Chouteau.

"Their village was attacked yesterday by a war party of

Pawnee, but that won't happen again, or at least not anytime soon," stated Gabriel.

Chouteau frowned, "Pawnee? This far south? That's unusual. We've traded with them at our posts on the Missouri, but never seen them this far south." He turned to Bear, "Did your people suffer much loss?"

"Two were killed, a few were hurt, but many Pawnee will not return to their people."

Chouteau scowled, "Is your village near?"

"Yes."

Chouteau let a slow grin cross his face since he knew the Osage to be less than forthcoming in their conversations and chose not to press Bear for any more information, but said, "If you return to your village soon, tell them we are anxious to start trading with them, and we have many goods to trade."

"Well, as far as trading goes, how 'bout we get some supplies and get back on our way?" suggested Gabriel, rising from the chair and tossing the dregs of the coffee in the bushes. The others followed his example and they walked to the fort, leading their horses, to begin the deal.

As they gathered their staples and goods together, Gabriel added a few extra items for Honey Bear, wanting her outfitted for the winter, although she did not know he was getting those things for her. Once outside, as they were packing the additional goods in the panniers and parfleches, she was surprised when the laid two blankets over the back of her horse and added a tin of powder, a bar of lead, and other items. She frowned and asked, "Why do you put that on my horse?"

"That's to help you get prepared for winter. You haven't had time to get goods to trade, and since you've spent your time helping us, it's only right that we share with you."

"I am coming with you," she said rather assertively.

"You're what?" asked Gabriel, stunned.

She laughed, putting her hand to her mouth as she continued, rocking back on her heels as she pointed at the expression on Gabriel's face, then explained. "My people want us to meet them for the buffalo hunt. They asked me to bring you," she nodded to both Gabriel and Ezra, "to hunt with them. It is a great honor. You must come." Gabriel exhaled the breath he didn't realize he was holding, letting his shoulders slump, and Bear laughed again. She gave him a coy smile and cocked her head slightly and looked at Gabriel, "Do you not want Bear to come with you?"

Gabriel slowly shook his head, letting a grin show, and answered, "Don't go acting cute with me, you know what I was thinking! I'm not ready to take a wife!"

Ezra was laughing with Bear and added, "But Gabe, winter's coming!"

All three laughed together, but the look in Honey Bear's eyes was a little mysterious, even for a woman.

20 / Buffalo

"There's a fresh cut trail 'tween here and the Verdigris!" proclaimed Chouteau. "Soon's we're done with this 'un, we'll be takin' a load o' goods there. If you find yourself wantin' something to do, you can always ride along and help protect the goods."

"That's a mighty temptin' offer, Mr. Chouteau, but we'll be huntin' buffalo with the Osage. If the migration route of the buffalo is not too far from the Verdigris, we might swing by the post 'n see if there's anybody ready to trade," replied Gabriel.

"You do that! Even if the post hasn't been built, there should be a trader there with at least a couple wagons of goods."

"You won't be there?" asked Ezra.

"No, no. I'll be back in St. Louis. There's much to do there," answered Chouteau.

"Then perhaps we'll see you again, but not anytime soon," suggested Gabriel.

It was just after midday when the trio left Fort Carondelet, bound for the buffalo migration route and the last hunt of the season for the Osage people. They rode into the sun, staying north of the Little Osage River, but when it turned and ran from north to south, they crossed, and soon made camp on the lee side of a long ridge of buttes that rose about two hundred feet above their location. With ample supply of both deer and bear meat, although they had left some with the people in the Osage village, there was no need to hunt, and all pitched in to quickly make camp. The horses were hobbled and given free graze of the wide meadow below them, and the small fire was nestled under a big elm that stretched its thick but leafless branches to disperse what little smoke that came from the dry wood.

Bear had assumed the cooking duties and Ezra and Gabriel gladly condescended, enjoying fresh coffee as they watched her. Gabriel's thoughts took a turn when he looked at Bear, thinking of her as a woman rather than a freed captive. She was beautiful, and her trim figure and gentle features belied her strength and abilities. Every move was deliberate and graceful, and her cheerful countenance added to her beauty. Her long black hair, hanging in two braids that were decorated with colorful strips of cloth, shone in the evening light with the sheen of a raven's wing. And whenever she passed near, Gabriel couldn't help but breathe deep of her essence, which reminded him of a combination of columbine and wild milkweed. She smiled often, and he couldn't help but smile back.

It was obvious she had noticed his attention and enjoyed it, making a point of passing close beside him and even touching him as she moved around the fire. She had a venison stew with potatoes, onions, and yampa root simmering over the low-burning fire and she stirred it often, requiring her to pass by Gabriel on each occasion. She poured both men more coffee and handed them a tin to start dishing up the stew. When they sat back and dug in, both men smiled broadly, and Ezra said, "Mmmm, this is mighty fine!"

Bear smiled, handed him a johnnycake, and dished up her own tin of stew. She sat back beside Gabriel, the short log making them sit close enough to be touching, but neither chose to move. Gabriel caught a grin from Ezra, and a blush rose up his neck and across his cheeks as he quickly took another bite of stew and johnnycake.

After dinner, as they sat back enjoying the cool of the evening, Gabriel asked Bear, "You spoke of Wah-kon-tah as the Great Spirit, but you learned about Jesus from the black robes. What do you believe about God?"

"Are they not the same? Your God is everywhere. So too is Wah-kon-tah," replied Bear.

"Yes, but God is not just everywhere, he is personal with man. That's why we know Jesus, who is God in the flesh. You see, Bear, when we do wrong, that's called sin. And sin has a penalty, which is death and eternity in Hell. But God provided a way out, and that way is Jesus. Does Wah-kon-tah do that?" asked Ezra.

"No. I have wondered about that, and about what happens

after we die. The black robes spoke of Heaven but did not tell us how to get there. What I understood from them was that one must do as the black robes told us, and maybe we would see Heaven. But how can we know for sure?" asked Bear.

"That's why God sent Jesus. He died on the cross to pay the price for our sins and to give us a gift of eternal life in Heaven. When we believe that in our hearts and ask God for that gift, He gladly gives it to us. But more than that, when we receive that gift, which is accepting Jesus into our lives, He changes us, and we are what the Bible calls born again. That means we are different because of Jesus in our lives."

"Different how?" asked Bear, curious but not understanding. Although she had a basic knowledge of Christianity from her childhood with the black robes, the teaching of the Little Old Ones, the spiritual leaders of her people, although similar, held many differences.

"Because He is in our lives, we have that presence and knowledge that guides us *if* we yield ourselves to Him. And of course, as we learn about Him through His Bible and spend time with Him in prayer, we become more like Him," explained Ezra.

"This gift...how do we get it?" inquired Bear.

"The gift of eternal life told about in Romans 6:23, 'The gift of God is eternal life through Jesus Christ our Lord,' must be received. We must ask for it and accept it. We do that when we believe in our hearts that it is true and is for us, then we ask in prayer. That is told in Romans 10:9-10, 'That if thou shalt confess with thy mouth the Lord Jesus, and shalt believe in thine heart that God hath raised him from the dead, thou shalt be saved. For with the heart man believeth unto righteousness and with the mouth confession is made unto salvation.'"

"Will you show me how to pray?" asked Bear timidly, looking to Ezra from the corner of her eye.

Ezra glanced at Gabriel, then back at Bear and smiled, "Of course. We'll pray together, and you can pray as I do, but only if you mean it in your heart." He began with a prayer of thanksgiving for God showing them the way of the Scripture, then he led Bear in a simple request to ask God to forgive her for her sins, and to come into her heart and give her the free gift of eternal life and to help her learn and grow in her Christian life. They ended with an "Amen" and smiled and laughed together, relieved to know for certain that an eternity in Heaven awaited them all.

The rest of the evening was spent with all three asking questions, finding answers, learning, and sharing their thoughts and concerns regarding life and their future, but the heavy weight of uncertainty had been lifted, and a new spirit prevailed. With lighter hearts, the three crawled into their blankets, looked to the star-filled heavens, and prayed their individual prayers of thanksgiving.

The morning sky was dimpled with a smattering of grey clouds whose gold bellies contrasted with the dusty colors of the tops. Overhead, the wispy and thin clouds carried fine lines of color that soon dissipated as the sun crested the eastern horizon. The three rode with the sun to their backs, moving single-file through the trees. They had rounded the shoulder of the ridge and held to the flats with the random meadows and tree cover. Bear had explained the usual migratory route of the buffalo was between the Neosho and Verdigris Rivers, but that varied with the whims of the herd leaders.

It was midday of the third day out of Carondelet when they crossed the Neosho, and they had yet to see any sign of the herds. "The buffalo start their journey south after the first snowfall. If we do not see their sign, we will move north to find them," said Bear. But less than an hour later, they crested a timber-covered bluff and spotted the slow-moving, casually grazing mass of buffalo. Appearing as a thick brown blanket for as far as they could see, the air was filled with the reek of dung and the clatter of horns and hooves and the grunts of the beasts. The men had never seen the like and stood beside their mounts, mesmerized by the sight. They could not imagine what a hunt would be like with the many Osage moving among the beasts and their minds filled with images of their own involvement. Gabriel looked at Ezra, "This is gonna be somethin'!"

"Ummhmm, but I'm not sure just how we're gonna do it!" answered his friend.

Bear grinned as she looked at the two men, "My people have hunted the buffalo for many generations. We will show you what to do against the beast of the prairie."

"Then how 'bout we make camp down below this bluff while we wait for your people?" directed Gabriel.

They moved into the shadow of the low-rising bluff, knowing the hill and thick trees offered all the cover they would need. The bison prefer to stay in the open grasslands, trusting their speed and size to overcome their poor eyesight. Their camp was made, and the horses picketed in a short while, and Gabriel walked with Honey Bear into the flats, taking in the sights of the plains. He walked with his open hands at his sides, feeling the tops of the different grasses, most bowing heavy heads with their packets of seeds. He recognized the tall, skinny Indian grass, the slightly shorter bluestem, and the bushy arrowfeather. There were other strains he did not recognize, but the bounty of grass moved with the breeze like the waves of the oceans, wave upon wave and as far as he could see, never-ending.

Bear watched the white man who had become so much a part of her life, enjoying his discovery and fascination with the plains. She spoke softly, "That," nodding to the waves of grass, "is why my people believe in Wah-kon-tah, the Great Spirit power who moves upon all living things. They believe he brings the buffalo to us in the time of greening, and again before the time of snows. All living things are Wah-kon-tah."

"It is the same with us, but we believe God is the power and the spirit that moves and controls everything, but He does more and chooses for us to have a personal closeness and knowledge of Him," answered Gabriel.

Bear smiled, reached for his hand, and held it as they walked, "I believe that too, now. I am happy to know that your God is also my God."

Gabriel squeezed her hand in his and turned to walk back to their camp. As they drew near, Ezra descended from the low knoll and pointed to the east, "Your people are coming. Looks like the whole village!"

Bear smiled, "All the people of the village, but a few very old ones, will be here for this hunt. The warriors will kill the buffalo, and the women and children will do the rest. But all will have a part."

21 / Camp

"I told you he was a tracker! That man could track a lizard across a hot rock!" declared Frank, slapping Frenchy on the shoulder.

After three days of wandering and wondering, Bucky Ledbetter had reported back with a broad grin and stood in his stirrups, "Found 'em!"

"Where?" growled Frank as he scowled at the one tracker in his bunch.

Bucky sat back and stuffed some tobacco in his corncob pipe, stepped down to the fire and used a stick to light the pipe, exhaled, and then answered, "They left a trail after leavin' that cave they holed up in. Went straight to a Injun village. That's where they was when I left this mornin'. But that ain't no little village like the last 'un."

"What tribe?" asked Frenchy.

"Don't rightly know. I heerd tell of them Osage an' how they was taller'n most. Must be them, 'cuz I seen some mighty big Injuns. An' that ain't all. They musta had a run-in with some other'ns, 'cuz they was a bunch o' dead ones piled up in a crick in the trees," explained Bucky, taking a draw on his pipe and letting the smoke slowly escape and slide through his whiskers and up beside his nose.

"But you're sure that Stonecroft and his negra are with 'em?" snarled Frank.

"Yup, they was when I left. But there's sumpin' else you might wanna know. That Injun village has a bunch o' poles outside of it, and there's a head of a Injun on each pole!"

"You're crazy! Ain't no Injuns do that! They scalp their enemies; they don't take off their heads! Why, that's barbaric!" declared Frenchy, astounded by the description given by Bucky.

Bucky just looked at him and took another draw on his pipe. Then, looking at Frank, he said, "You might wanna watch yore friend there. He as much as called me a liar, an' I don't take that from no man. If he weren't yore friend, he'd be buzzard bait 'bout now." Bucky stood, went to his horse, loosened the girth, and led the animal to water. He thought it best that he put some distance between him and Frenchy before something else was said and somebody died.

Squirrel looked at Frenchy and whined, "I ain't never seen Bucky let a man talk like that. You're lucky you ain't dead!"

Frenchy looked at Frank, and the big man nodded, "He's right. That man might not look like trouble to you, but I've seen him lay out others for less. Might wanna watch your step around him."

"Well, you don't believe what he said about those heads, do you?" asked Frenchy.

"Why would he lie about somethin' like that? What difference does it make, anyway?" answered Frank. "You stay here. I'm gonna ask him how far that village is and what he thinks about gettin' those two."

Bucky was sitting on the grassy bank of the small creek, looking at some minnows swimming against the current when Frank came to his side. The big man sat down next to him and asked, "So, how far is that village?"

"Took me a day an' a half to come back. If we get an early start, might make it in a long day."

"Think we can get those two away from the Injuns?" asked Frank, tossing a stone in the creek and watching the minnows scatter.

"Dunno. The sign I followed showed they picked up 'nother'n. Coulda been a wanderin' brave or a woman, hard to say. But their tracks was wiped out by the bunch what attacked the village. When I got there, it was gettin' on dark, an' I waited till mornin' so's I could see. Took some doin', but I spotted that big black horse first, then saw that tow-headed white boy comin' outta one o' them bark lodges. Oncet I saw him, I high-tailed it back to you'ns."

"You done good, Bucky, real good." Frank started to leave, then sat back down, "Don't pay much attention to that Frenchy. He ain't gonna be with us long nohow." Grinning, he stood to leave.

"When you git ready to dismiss him, let me be for doin' it,

what say?" asked Bucky.

"You got it."

*   *   *   *   *

Gabriel and Ezra were fascinated as they watched the village of the Osage rise from the plains. Teepees rose, first the tripod of poles, then others laid in place, followed by the drawing of the hide covering to the top and spread across the skeleton of poles. Lodge after lodge grew from the grass, all erected by the women with the entry facing east, and each taking its place in relation to those of the leaders. Children were tasked with carrying the parfleches and other parcels that had been carried on the travois behind the camp dogs, into the erected lodges. Older youngsters tended to the herd of horses while men prepared their weapons for the hunt. Bear had joined her people and was helping those of her extended family with their duties.

The two men, seated near their fire ring and drinking their coffee, had a panoramic view from the slight rise that held their camp near the tree line. "You know, that's the way things should be done. No one standing around barking orders, just everyone knowing their job and doing it. You don't see that too often back in civilization!" declared Gabriel.

"That's 'cuz the *important* people are more concerned about who's the boss and who gets the credit. That's why it takes the government twice as long and costs twice as much to get the same thing done that others can do in less time!" surmised Ezra.

Gabriel chuckled, then motioned with his chin toward the village, "Here comes Bear and some o' the others." Five men accompanied Bear to the camp of Gabriel and Ezra. Led by Blue Corn, the recognized leader of the council called the Little Old Ones, the group stopped as they neared the two friends. Both men stood and waited for the leader to speak.

"We come to ask you to join us for the hunt," spoke Blue Corn. Bear stood to the side, watching Gabriel to see if he understood the chief, who spoke in the Osage dialect of the Algonquin language, but also in sign. A slight nod from Gabriel told her he understood as he watched the chief sign.

Gabriel replied in his limited Osage, also using sign, "We would be honored to join you." He motioned for the group to be seated but the chief shook his head, motioning for them to follow him and the others. Honey Bear stepped beside Gabriel and spoke softly, "We will scout the herd from atop the bluff," she said, motioning to the trail through the trees to the bluff top.

As they neared the crest of the bald bluff, everyone went into a crouch and then to their bellies as they looked at the herd on the flats before them. Blue Corn was beside the war leader, Eagle's Wing, and they spoke softly, motioning to the herd and the surrounding terrain. The leaders scooted backward, and once below the crest, they sat up, looking at the others. Eagle's Wing spoke, "Those that hunt mounted will go with me to the far side. Those who use rifles will go with Blue Corn and come to the herd from the creek bed." He looked at Gabriel, "Will you hunt mounted?"

"That I will," he answered.

Eagle's Wing looked at Ezra, who answered, "No, I'll use my rifle. It's kinda hard to reload on horseback, and I might need more'n one shot." Bear translated and the others grinned, nodding agreement.

When the chief and war leader looked at the others for any comments, no one spoke, and Eagle's Wing finally said, "Before first light." They all nodded or grunted, then stood and started down the trail through the trees. The remaining light would be used to prepare for the hunt, the men tending to weapons and their preferred horse, the women sharpening knives and preparing the travois for hauling the meat and hides. Gabriel, Ezra, and Bear were also busy in their camp, cleaning weapons and making ready for the morrow.

Gabriel looked at Bear, "Will you be in the hunt or . . ."

She smiled, "I am a proven warrior of my people, so I can hunt with the other warriors. But you," nodding to both men, "will need someone to tend to your kills, so I have chosen that work."

Gabriel scowled, "I figgered we'd tend to our own kills. You don't have to do that."

"I know, but it is my way of honoring you. I have a friend who will help. Her man was killed in the attack, and she will need meat for the winter. She is called Grey Fox, and she has two little ones who must be cared for also."

"Good, because I'm certain that we," he motioned to himself and Ezra, "won't be able to use a whole buffalo, much less more'n one." He looked at Bear, "So, are we supposed to shoot more than one?"

Bear smiled, "Yes, because what you do not use will go to the rest of the village, and they will need much meat for the winter. Grey Fox will come here soon to help with a travois."

Gabriel was finishing some arrows, painting the shafts black with a concoction made from charcoal, chokecherry juice, and bear fat. He had filed some metal points to a razor-sharp edge before binding them to the shaft with fine sinew and the fletching was from turkey feathers, making the entire arrow dark and unique from those used by the Osage. He held one up, examining the straightness of the shaft, and Bear asked, "Why is it so long?"

Gabriel grinned, "You saw my bow. When I bring it to full draw, I must have a long arrow. These," nodding toward the completed arrows, "are a little more than a hand's-breadth longer than the usual arrow."

"You will not use your rifle tomorrow?"

"Oh, I'll have it with me, but like Ezra said, it is hard to reload horseback. I can do just as well with the bow, maybe even better."

Their attention was diverted by Grey Fox coming to their camp, leading a bay horse pulling a travois. She smiled as she neared and Bear called out, "Grey Fox! Good of you to come." Bear went to her friend, and they embraced before Bear led her into their camp. She did not appear to be more than twenty, and the two youngsters that followed her, one about five or so and the other a curious and rambunctious three. Fox was a pretty woman with the typical long hair and dark eyes, but her smile was constant, and her eyes sparkled with mischief. Although not slender, she filled out her dress well. Her cheeks appeared like shiny crabapples, and her hands were always busy, first with the horse, then with the travois, always moving as the two women chattered.

Ezra watched the women as they worked, and Gabriel watched Ezra. It was evident the woman had caught his eye, and he seemed intrigued by her. The children were busy with sticks and a rock they batted to one another, and Ezra lay his cleaned rifle aside to pour himself another cup of coffee. It was an enjoyable evening that reminded them of times at home with family. But the night grew dark and cool, prompting Fox and children to return to the village and their lodge. When she was gone, Ezra asked Bear, "What happens to a woman of your people when she loses her husband?"

"It is not unlike your people. The woman is free to take another mate or to stay alone, but among our people, because she is of the Tzi-sho, the People of the Sky, she can only marry a man from the Hun-Kah, the People of the Land, or from outside the tribe. The village cares for the old and the women who have no man, sharing what they have with each one. Grey Fox will have her brother to help with the children. It is common for the brother of the woman to do the training of the children, more so than the father," explained Bear, looking at Ezra with a slight grin. "Does she appeal to you?"

Ezra dropped his gaze to the fire, squirmed on his seat, and said, "She *is* a very attractive woman."

Gabriel and Bear grinned, and Bear replied, "She

thinks you are a good man and that you are strong, and hopes you are a good hunter."

"Hopes?" scowled Ezra.

"Yes. A woman always wants a man who is a good hunter and can provide for her lodge."

"Now, hold on there! I just said she was attractive. That don't mean I'm thinkin' marriage!" responded a frustrated Ezra.

Gabriel and Bear again laughed at his response and began preparing their bedrolls for the night, chuckling all the while. Ezra, mumbling and grumbling, tossed his blankets around and dropped down to stretch out and try to get some sleep before the early rise for the hunt. As he lay still, his mind turned to the image of Grey Fox, and he fought his blankets as he tried to make sense of his thoughts.

22 / Hunt

The mounted hunters moved quietly around the long bluff, staying in the thinning timber. Once south of the dropped shoulder of the ridge, timber became scarce, but the low swale gave them cover in the dim light of early morning. The grey line that silhouetted the eastern horizon made faint but long shadows of the hunters. With the only sounds the muted footfalls of the horses and the faint creak of leather, the occasional snort of an anxious mount, and the covered cough of a rider, the line of twenty-two hunters appeared as ghostly waifs in the low-lying fog that rose from the river behind them. The horses waded through the grassy mist, their noses pushing it before them.

Led by Eagle's Wing with his brother White Crow following, Gabriel was given a place of honor as third in the long line of hunters. These men would use the weapons of the ancients, bows and arrows and lances. To hunt from horseback with these weapons, the buffalo must be to the left of the horses since the natural shooting of the bow was with the weapon in the left hand and the right hand drawing the string with the nocked arrow held across his body. Likewise, with the lance thrown with the right hand across the body to take the animal on the left. Most rode horses experienced and proven in the hunt, while Gabriel had used his bow from horseback just the one time during the Pawnee attack. But he was confident in the big black, who stood taller than all the Indian ponies, most coming from wild herds but still descended from horses not unlike Ebony, that came from the Spaniards. Their horses stood between fourteen hands and fifteen-two, while Ebony was easily measured at sixteen hands, with his proud carriage and arched neck making him appear even taller.

The other hunters admired the big stallion, and when given the chance, expressed their appreciation of the gallant steed. Gabriel often leaned down and stroked the black's neck, speaking softly to him to keep him calm and steady. If given his head, the black would charge to the front of the line for his nature was to lead and run at the head of any herd. Now Gabriel sought to calm him, wanting to focus on the hunt, for he would be running at full tilt alongside a herd of beasts where each animal weighed twice as much and wouldn't hesitate to try to gut him with their horns. Gabriel knew his horse and felt he was an extension of him. He was confident he could easily guide him with nothing more than leg pressure, but in the excitement of the hunt, any animal could become frightened and unmanageable.

They had followed the south fork of the Neosho, staying in the thin timber, to make their way to the western edge of the herd. A small stream that fed the south fork came from the north, and the creek-side brush offered ample cover for the hunters. They needed to get at least midway of the herd; too far out in front and they would be trampled, and too far back would put them in danger of the herd bulls that looked for anything to tangle with and pushed the herd in any stampede or sudden jump for the migration.

As they rode, Wing motioned to Gabriel to come alongside, then pointed to a swath of ground that was almost devoid of grass but had several mounds of dirt. He spoke in English as he pointed, "That is a village of the *Móonack,* what the white man calls 'prairie dog.' If the buffalo come this way, do not follow. Your horse will step in the holes and break his leg." Gabriel nodded in understanding and dropped back to his place in line. Once in position, the men dropped to the ground, waiting for the shooters across the herd to be ready.

"How will you know they are ready?" asked Gabriel, standing near Eagle's Wing.

The war leader motioned with his chin toward the bluff they'd used the day before for their scout, "Standing Elk will be there, praying, and he will send smoke. Then when I say we are ready, we will send an arrow high to start the hunt."

Gabriel smiled and pulled one of the whistling arrows from his quiver to show Wing, "This is a whistling arrow. I can shoot it high enough and far enough that the others will hear it if they can't see it."

Wing looked at the arrow and watched as Gabriel swung it back and forth to demonstrate the whistle, although it was much less than it would make in flight. Wing scowled and reached for the arrow to examine it closely. He looked at Gabriel and nodded, as anxious to hear the whistling arrow as to see the white man use his unusual bow.

Blue Corn led the shooters as they walked within the tree line, working their way north and paralleling the meandering Neosho River. Once in position near the middle of the length of the herd, he motioned to the others, and they dropped to hands and knees to move through the tall Indian and bluestem grass nearer the herd. They would have no protection if the herd chose to move in their direction, so it was imperative they started the hunt with rifle shots rather than allow the mounted hunters to push the herd toward them. The eighteen shooters were spaced five to ten yards apart in a single line along the eastern edge of the herd. When Blue Corn stopped, the word was passed in whispers for the shooters to stop their advance and be ready with their chosen shots. No one was to open fire until after Blue Corn.

The chief lifted slowly up to look back toward the bluff where Standing Elk was to be watching. He slowly raised the muzzle of his rifle that had a feather near the front sight for Elk to see and be ready to send his smoke for the other hunters. Within moments, he saw the thin spiral of grey lift above the trees, catching the rising sun and shimmering with the pinks and oranges of the morning light. Blue Corn rose to a sitting position, his elbows on his knees as he searched for a cow without a calf at her side. He located what he wanted, and with the front blade sight cutting the buckhorn rear sight, he eared back the hammer to ready his shot. But his eyes lifted when he heard a strange whistle high above the herd. A few of the animals looked side to side, but none were alarmed. A rambunctious orange calf jumped and kicked as he ran toward another, butting it and bouncing back, challenging the other calf to a bout.

Blue Corn resumed his sighting, and with his finger on the thin trigger, he slowly squeezed. The rifle roared, bucked, and spat smoke and fire as it sent the ball to its mark. The sudden blast and the snort and buck of the cow startled the herd, and the entire mass of brown and black moved as if connected by an invisible tether, lunging forward and starting the stampede. Other rifles roared instantly after the first shot, and more animals stumbled, staggered, and fell. Some limped away as they sought to keep up with the herd.

The shooters began frantically reloading as the thundering herd made even the ground beneath them vibrate and rumble. The bellowing and snorting of the cows and bulls, the bleating of frightened calves, and the clatter of horns and hooves made the men think of the thundering of a massive storm that rolled overhead instead of underfoot. Dust clouds rose as much from the dirt in the shaggy coats of the brown beasts as from the trampled soil and torn grasses that had fed the melee just moments before.

Ezra had scored with his first shot and the carcass lay

less than forty yards directly in front of him, but the rising cloud of dust obscured the animal as the herd rumbled past. He extracted the ramrod, laid it at his side, and filled the pan, then dropped the frizzen and cocked the hammer as he searched for his next target. He saw a lumbering cow, tongue lolling and head swinging, and he brought his sights to bear, squeezed off his shot, and saw her stumble, chin on the ground as she slid to a stop. He instantly started reloading, and with one eye on his rifle and the other on the herd, watched for another target.

When Gabriel sent the whistling arrow aloft, the nearby hunters watched the arrow arc and stood in awe as they heard the whistle that sounded like the constant scream of a red-shouldered hawk as it disappeared beyond the herd. Gabriel marked where it went, thinking he could retrieve it after the hunt. Once the whistle had died, every hunter swung aboard his mount, reaching for their weapons and the rattle of rifle fire and the lunge of the herd started them on their way.

The horde of hunters drove straight at the side of the running herd, and as they neared, they swung alongside, matching the pace of the beasts stride for stride. Eagle's Wing sat slightly hunched along the neck of his mount as he brought his bow to full draw and loosed his first arrow to impale itself in the side of a big cow. The bison stumbled but kept running, and the war leader launched another arrow to sink next to the first, just behind the right front shoulder of the cow, causing it to stagger and bury its nose in the dirt, flipping end over end.

Gabriel had watched the war leader, then chose his own target. A good-sized cow, not massive but sizable, showing she was young and tender. Gabriel nudged Ebony, who was running all-out, a little nearer with leg pressure as he brought the Mongol bow to full draw, then he shot the arrow that went deep into the chest of the cow at a downward angle behind the front shoulder. The cow made two strides and dropped as if her legs had been jerked from under her, sliding on her chin and chest to plow a furrow as she came to a stop.

The big black had not missed a step and stretched out, overtaking White Crow, and as Gabriel guided him, he moved alongside a young bull, allowing Gabriel to score another kill with the long black arrow that buried itself in the neck of the beast. He dropped his head in the dirt and rolling over in a heap, caused the cow behind him to jump clear. Gabriel nocked another arrow since Ebony now had the gait of the hunt mastered, and they searched for another target. A quick glance toward the leader and Gabriel saw a big cow, head lowered in a charge, gaining on the war leader's horse, but Wing was unaware of the danger behind him. Gabriel urged the black to a faster run, asking him to stretch out and move as only he could, and the stallion eagerly responded with his long strides. They came beside the cow, who saw the threat at her side and lowered her head to try to hook the stallion. Gabriel loosed the arrow that quickly pierced the thick hide and wooly coat of the buffalo and disappeared into the side of the charging beast, making her stumble and lift her head. With another arrow quickly nocked, Gabriel readied his shot and sent the arrow into the cow, dropping her. She fell and slid to a stop.

Gabriel glanced toward Wing and saw that the man twisted around to watch the white man kill the cow that was charging his horse. Without slowing, both men continued on their hunt and sought new targets. He looked at the head of the herd, saw they were nearing the south fork of the Neosho, and was reminded of the prairie dog village. He guided Ebony away from the herd, as did Wing and the others, to avoid the pitfall.

The herd continued running without slowing, pushed from behind by the herd bulls, who grunted, bellowed, and thundered past. The dust cloud moved like a desert thunderstorm, covering everything with a layer of fine brown dust as it settled over the land and the hunters. They watched as the rest of the herd passed, leaving behind the scarred prairie that appeared as a freshly turned piece of farmland, with the only blossoms being the carcasses of their kills.

At a shout from one of the mounted warriors, they followed his lead as he went to the nearest downed buffalo. He dropped to the ground, kicked at the carcass, and, seeing no movement drew out his knife and began splitting the gut of the beast. The other hunters came to the side of the first, and as he dragged the steaming innards from the cow, he worked with his knife and laid open the liver and the gall bladder. He stood, screamed his victory shout to the sky, and bit into the liver, now covered with the bile from the bladder. Blood streamed from the corners of his mouth as he passed the big dark-red organ to the man next to him. The act was repeated again and again as the liver was passed from man to man.

When it came to Gabriel, everyone watched as he duplicated the act, taking a big bite, cutting the piece with his knife just in front of his nose, and chomping down on the raw meat.

He nodded to the others as he chewed, watching the remaining hunters take their portions. With every hunter sated, the tidbit that was left was handed to the war leader, Eagle's Wing, and he quickly devoured the meager morsel. The men wiped their faces on their sleeves and mounted up to go to the individual kills, to claim each as his own. Gabriel pulled his arrows from the cow that had surrendered her liver to the ceremony, wiped them clean, and dropped them into his quiver. He looked up to see Eagle's Wing standing at the head of the animal, and the man said, "This one was charging my horse."

"Yeah, she was, and wanted to hook mine with her horns, but . . ." replied Gabriel as he put one foot on the shoulder of the dead cow and leaned forward with his hand on his knee. He looked down at the big wooly creature and added, "She's a big 'un!" Wing stepped toward Gabriel and extended his arm and the two clasped forearms, but the war leader pulled Gabriel closer and put his other arm around him and the men bumped shoulders, then pulled away. Wing said, "I owe you my life."

Gabriel dropped his gaze to the buffalo and replied, "You don't owe me anything, Eagle's Wing. It was an honor to join the hunt."

Ezra and the other shooters had walked to their kills, and the celebratory act of consuming the liver was repeated, led by Blue Corn. Ezra joined in, but with less enthusiasm than Gabriel, and was glad when the others dispersed to their kills. He knew he had dropped at least two, and maybe three, but with nothing but bullet holes to mark the kills, he just sat on the one directly opposite his shooting position and looked around at the other kills.

The women started from the trees, leading horses that trailed travois. Dogs with small travois followed, usually with a youngster beside them. There was much chattering as they approached each animal, some with shooters nearby, but others lying solitary. Ezra grinned when he saw Bear and Grey Fox coming toward him and said, "Well, I got this 'un." He pointed to two other carcasses nearby. "An' that 'un, an' that 'un. That enough?"

Both women nodded enthusiastically and quickly started on the first cow by splitting the hide from chin to tail and dragging out the innards. Ezra watched, learning, and asked, "What can I do?"

Bear grinned, "Take the travois off the horse, and we will use him to pull the carcass over to finish skinning."

And so it began, women doing most of the work, men helping as needed, but a jovial spirit prevailed as they delighted in the bountiful hunt. Nothing of the buffalo would be wasted; the larger bones would supply ample marrow, the hides everything from lodges to rawhide containers. Even the brains were used in the tanning of the leather. Once the work was done, there would be a feast of celebration to enjoy the fresh meat and what they viewed as the tastiest parts: the tongue, the heart, the liver, and more.

23 / Feast

Cookfires dotted the plains like candles on a cake, smoke rising in thin columns lifting their way toward the clear blue sky. Strips of meat hung dripping over the low-burning fires, offering tasty tidbits to all the workers and youngsters who scampered about. Wolves, coyotes, badgers, and more circled the killing grounds, darting in and out among the carcasses and people, snatching bits of entrails and castoffs. Turkey buzzards drifted on updrafts, dropping from the sky to claim the carrion, contesting with crows, ravens, hawks, and eagles. The women were unconcerned with the scrap eaters, believing Wah-kon-tah sent each one to do its part in the harvesting of the bounty.

Trek after trek was made, leading horses with the heavily laden travois to the encampment, where other women had already started cutting the meat into thin strips and laying them on the willow smoke racks that sat astraddle the smoldering hickory and maplewood fires. The women who finished their work on the killing field worked with the meat at the smoke fires, and together, they prepared the food for the feast.

A festive spirit filled the encampment, everyone participating in the preparations and sharing with one another. No one would go hungry this winter. When the warriors returned to a raucous welcome, the shouting and celebrating set the tone for the evening's activities. The men and women went to their lodges to put on their finery for the dances and the telling of the stories of the hunt. Gabriel and Ezra went to their camp to sit beside their small fire, relax, and share their tales with one another, but were surprised to see both Bear and Fox already at work. The women had built several smoke racks that were loaded with meat, and a large pot of stew was simmering on the fire.

"Howa!" said Bear, smiling at the returning hunters. Her greeting was echoed by Fox as she turned from laying strips on the smoke racks. Gabriel and Ezra both answered with "Howa!" as they stepped down from their horses.

"You ladies have been busy!" declared Gabriel, starting to strip the gear from Ebony.

"You great hunters killed many buffalo!" responded Bear, grinning. She was tending the stew at the fire and bent to pick up the coffee pot to pour each of the men a cup.

Ezra laughed, "So, does that mean we are truly great hunters?" he asked, remembering the remarks of the night before.

Fox said, "You two took more buffalo than any other hunters in the camp!" She smiled as she looked at the men.

"Well, it certainly looks like there's enough meat for us, and more besides," declared Gabriel.

Bear laughed, "This is but one buffalo," she told him, motioning to the racks and piles of meat. "We gave the others to the women of the village. We could not prepare it before it would go bad, but they will enjoy it all winter!"

"Well, good for you, and for them as well. It's great to know they will have a good winter." He accepted the offered cup and started to sit down, but saw Eagle's Wing walking to their camp and waited for his arrival. When the war leader neared, Gabriel asked, "Would you like some coffee?"

Wing smiled and nodded, accepted the offered cup, and sat on one of the logs Ezra had pulled to the fireside. Gabriel noticed the concerned expression on the man's face and sat down to wait for his words. He sipped the coffee, nodded his approval, and turned to Gabriel. "One of our young men who stayed at our village was at my lodge when we returned. He tells of some white men who came into our village, looking to find you. They said they were friends, but our people did not believe them. They were told you went to the trader's fort and they knew no more."

"Did he tell you how many or what they looked like?" asked Gabriel.

"One very big." He motioned with his hands to indicate tall and wide. "One small like badger, four others." He held up four fingers.

"Did they harm anyone in the village?" asked Ezra, concerned for the old people.

"No, they go to the fort. But our boy came, rode all night, to tell of them," explained Wing, sipping the hot coffee. It was a treat not often enjoyed because of its expense, but the man appreciated the offering. He dropped his gaze to the fire, waiting for Gabriel to explain. Although the way of the Osage was much like other natives; and they would not ask to be told about the others but would give the opportunity for sharing.

Gabriel began, "Wing, these are bad men. They want to kill me because another man offered a bounty on my life. Because Ezra travels with me, they would kill him also. The one who offers the bounty does so because I killed his son in a duel. Do you know about duels?"

"I have heard about the white man's way of shooting at one another."

"Well, that man spoke badly of my sister, and I stopped him. He challenged me to a duel but didn't follow the rules, and I had to kill him. Because of that, his father wants me dead and has offered to pay a good sum of money to see it done. That is why these men come after me. I do not want to bring this on your people, so Ezra and I will leave first thing in the morning if not before."

"You do not need to leave. If you stay, you will be safe among us. There are too many warriors for that small band of men," declared Wing indignantly.

"No, these men do not care who might be hurt. I don't want that for your people. It is better if we are away from the women and children, so no one else is killed."

Ezra had sat quiet and nodded in agreement when Wing looked his way. The war leader stood, "I will go with you or have some of my warriors to go with you if you say the word."

Shaking his head, Gabriel replied, "No, but thanks, Wing. You are a good friend, and I hope to come back to your village someday. Give my thanks to your leaders and your people for their kindness and the honor of joining your hunt. We are grateful."

Wing nodded, and the two friends clasped forearms and drew one another near, then stepped back as Wing left their camp. When Gabriel turned to the fire, he saw the women standing and watching, stoic expressions painted on their faces. They dropped their eyes and returned to their tasks. Gabriel sat back down and refilled his cup, then turned to Ezra, "So, what do you think?"

Ezra snorted, "Oh, they'll go to the fort all right, but who-ever's there will tell 'em we went on the buffalo hunt with the Osage. So, I reckon they'll be along in a day or so."

"That's just what I thought. Do you wanna leave tonight or wait till mornin'?"

Ezra paused, thinking, then looked up at Gabriel, "If we left tonight and followed that herd of buffalo a ways, then cut out in some creek or other, we might cover our trail enough to slow 'em down a little. But, I ain't too happy about runnin'. I'd rather do the attackin' instead of defendin', wouldn't you?"

"I think you're right on both points. We can get away from the Osage camp, maybe give ourselves some time by maskin' our trail, and then work out a plan to strike at them 'fore they catch up to us," agreed Gabriel.

Bear walked over to where Gabriel was seated and dropped down beside him. She looked at him and asked, "You would go without me?"

Gabriel wasn't surprised at the question, and he reached for Bear's hand, looked at the fire, and said, "It's not that I want to go without you, Bear, but these are killers of men, and they would not hesitate to kill you. I don't want that. It is best that Ezra and I leave, deal with these men, and hopefully return. I don't want to endanger you or your people, and this is *my* problem."

She waited for a moment, then put her other hand atop their clasped hands and asked, "And Ezra? Would he go without Fox? I have seen the way he looks at her, and she is pleased that he does. She is drawn to him."

Ezra was close enough to hear Bear's question, and said, "Yes, I see Fox as a very desirable woman, and I would like to have her with me, but I agree with Gabe. We do not want to put either of you in danger. It is best that we leave."

"But we could help." She sat up straight, "I am a warrior of the Ni-u-kon-ska, and I will fight for my man. Fox is skilled with the bow and the lance; she has fought by her man's side."

Both Gabriel and Ezra smiled at the remark, and Gabriel answered, "Yes, but if we were in a battle, I would be thinking about you and would not fight as well. As you know, a warrior must be focused only on the fight, or he will be killed."

Bear knew the words were true and knew she would also be more concerned about her man than the fight at hand. When a warrior fights, if he is intent on his battle, he is a fierce warrior, but if his attention is divided, he is less of a fighter. Bear looked at Gabriel and then to Ezra, sucked in a deep breath that lifted her shoulders, and stood. She looked back at Gabriel and said, "We go to the feast." With a motion to Fox, the two women took the pot of stew, carrying it between them, and started to the encampment of the Osage.

Ezra was reminded by the array of food set out for the feast of the many dinners that had been held at his father's church. It was a celebratory time, and the dances began with both warriors and women arrayed in their finery. Women sported dresses of white buckskin decorated heavily with beads, bells, quills, and more. Men prided themselves on the bangles in their ears and adorning their tunics, feathers that spoke of valor and bravery and accomplishments in battle, and gourds and rattles for the dance. Most dances were either the men or the women, but occasionally, they were together, and danced around the circle hand in hand. But Gabriel, Ezra, Bear, and Fox did not take part. While the mood of the people was one of rejoicing for the bountiful hunt, the four who sat near the lodge of Eagle's Wing were somber and stoic.

After they feasted, they watched the dances for a short while, but as the curtain of twilight fell, they rose and started for their camp. Bear and Fox walked beside them, seldom speaking, but treasuring the moments together. While the women filled two parfleches with the smoked meat, the men saddled the horses and checked their gear. Earlier, they had cleaned and loaded their rifles and pistols and repaired the packsaddles. Now, with the horses and packhorses geared up, they stepped before the women to say their goodbyes.

Thoughts of the future, its possibilities and perils, are not limited to those that reside in safety of their homes or lodges. These four friends had spent many moments considering their futures, both together and apart. The age-old call of home and hearth beckoned to Gabe and Ezra, but concern and caution set those thoughts aside as they contemplated what might lay in store. But now they must say their goodbyes. A farewell to those that were appreciated and even loved, howbeit never fulfilled. And with the danger that threatened, perhaps will never know fulfillment.

They looked at one another, embraced and held each other close. Then pushing apart, the men stepped aboard their horses, reined around and left. Neither man willing to look back at the women, knowing they might be tempted to change their mind and endanger them. They rode away, trailing the packhorses, and looking to the north star for guidance.

24 / Ruse

The sliver of moon hung lonesome in the dark sky. Random stars that had lit their lamps peeked from behind heavy clouds, and the world appeared as one big shadow. The flats were tall with Indian and bluestem grasses, intermingled with patches of the shorter grama and the bushy arrowfeather. The night breezes stirred the fading greenery with waves that beckoned the night travelers onward. Somewhere, a coyote sang his romantic calls, hoping for an answer, while cicadas drummed their rhythmic rattles, competing with the occasional bullfrog bragging about his territorial puddle.

The men were buried in somber thoughts, following the churned soil of the buffalo herd and enjoying the quickstep of the horses that rocked them in their saddles, making the leather add its own song to the darkness under the shifting weight of deep-thinking men. How quickly did the plans and dreams of men change upon the entry of women into their lives. When they left Philadelphia, neither man had considered the possibility of having a woman as part of their dreams. With thoughts of adventure and exploring the wild frontier, they had concerns about other things, setting aside the usual dreams of young men. But now both were bothered by the images and memories of women who had recently stepped into their thoughts and lives.

Gabriel had spoken with Eagle's Wing at length, quizzing him about the terrain and rivers before them, and asking about possible locations for an ambush or ways to escape. With that information fresh in his mind, after leaving the path of the herd, he pointed them almost due west. He wanted to reach the Verdigris river, perhaps at the location of Chouteau's second trading fort, and maybe further. Wing had suggested using the Verdigris or the Fall River, to confuse their followers, giving them time to set up an ambush or to attack their camp.

As he looked to the sky, he judged it to be just past midnight, and they stopped beside a small creek to give the horses a blow and for them to stretch their legs. Gabriel pulled out some smoked meat and sat on the grassy bank, feet toward the water, and when Ezra dropped beside him, he shared the meat. Ezra chomped down on the strip of jerky, tore off a piece, and began chewing, but spoke around the mass, "What would we do, traveling with women?" he asked, knowing both of them had been considering taking the women with them.

Gabriel cocked his head to the side and looked at his friend, "So, you been thinkin' about it, huh?"

Ezra chuckled and asked, "Haven't you?"

"Yeah, s'pose so, especially after Bear said she wanted to come with me. But with these bounty hunters after us, well..."

"I know. And every time I think about it, I see us traveling with two women and two youngsters and facing who knows what? Then I think I've only known her a few days, and I have to ask myself, what am I thinking?"

"They're both good cooks!" declared Gabriel, remembering.

Again, Ezra chuckled, "Ain't they, though?"

They sat for a while longer, eating their meat and thinking, then Ezra asked, "About these fellas followin' us. We know, or we think we know, that it's the same bunch we had a run-in with at New Madrid. So, do we just start shootin' or what?"

"We can't just start shooting, but neither do I want to be caught someplace where *they* just start shooting. I've been thinkin' about it, and if we get somewhere that we can maybe sneak up on 'em, find out for sure who they are and why they're following us, well, then we plan things a little differently. But we'll just have to play the cards we're dealt," suggested Gabriel.

"And that's what I don't like. We can't let them have control of whatever the situation might be, I still believe we need to take the offensive and do whatever we can to discourage 'em, even if that means killin' some of 'em."

Gabriel narrowed his eyes, "When we were back in Philadelphia, and even when we roamed through the woods, I never saw us killing men. Yet when we were on the river and were attacked by the river pirates and those who were bounty hunters, we dealt death quite easily. And that bothers me a little. Doesn't it you?"

Ezra stood and chucked a stone into the water, then faced his friend. "I don't see it that way. I mean, the idea of killing someone doesn't come easy to me, but when they're trying to kill me or friends of mine, it's the only thing we can do. This is a hard time we're living in, my friend, and it takes hard men to survive and work to make it a better place. When my father talked about the commandment, 'Thou shalt not kill,' he always explained that was to not murder someone. There's a big difference between killing for killing's sake and defending yourself. That's why God sent David against Goliath, knowing full well he would have to kill him, and many other times in the Bible where God's people brought death upon those who would do them harm. So no, it doesn't bother me when we have to kill to live."

Gabriel stood and put his hand on Ezra's shoulder, looked at him quite somberly, and said, "You'd make a good preacher! Have you ever thought about making the ministry your way of life?"

Ezra laughed, "You don't know how many times my father asked that question. Now, let's get a move on before I start another sermon!"

As the dark veil of night began to lift, the two friends approached the trees near the Verdigris River. Although most were naked and stood like skeletons in the dim light, a few clung tenaciously to their remaining leaves, appearing as if they were shaking blankets of brown-tinged leaves at the passersby. The leaves crunched underfoot as they neared the riverbank, and Gabriel reined up and leaned on the pommel to look at the river. His first look told of a river that was no more than eighty feet wide, and the ripples on the surface indicated shallow waters. He looked at Ezra, "Let's give the horses a chance to graze a little, and us too, and then we'll push on. I think we'll use this spot for what we got planned." He swung down and stripped the rig from Ebony, grabbing a handful of grass to rub him down.

Ezra, busy at rubbing down the bay, asked, "And just what is it *we* have planned?"

"You'll see, you'll see," answered Gabriel, grinning.

They took the time to make some coffee, heat up some leftover johnnycake, and cook some fresh meat. At Gabriel's suggestion, they stretched out for a short sleep, allowing the horses ample time for grazing and resting.

With the sun glaring, prying open his eyes, Gabriel rose, stretched, and shook Ezra awake. "Let's go, sleepyhead. We can sleep later!"

With Ezra grumbling all the while, they saddled up and started across the Verdigris River. It was an easy crossing and they rose up the opposite bank and moved through the thin trees into the flats a short distance when Gabriel stopped. "Now, let's go back to the trees, then we'll walk back and wipe out our trail." Ezra frowned, looked at his friend, and when Gabriel reined around, he followed.

Once back in the trees at a different location where the leaves were deep, Gabriel stepped down and tethered Ebony. "Now, follow my lead. We want to wipe out our trail and move through here across that neck of land where the river does a switchback on itself, then we'll stay in the water a spell before coming out upstream and headin' back west."

"Oh, is that all? Why, that's nothin'," replied Ezra, sarcastically.

Both men grabbed a branch that still had some leaves, then walked back to their turnaround. They gradually brushed out their tracks, making it appear the tracks gradually disappeared. Then with Ezra brushing, Gabriel gathered handfuls of dry soil and small debris and sifted it through his fingers, letting it fall naturally to the ground to mask the brush marks from the branches. Once back in the trees, he had Ezra lead the horses to the riverbank as he followed, kicking the leaves up and making it appear they had not been disturbed.

They entered the river again, moving across at a sharp angle and coming out well upstream of where they'd entered. They crossed the narrow neck of land where the river did a sharp cutback on itself, then re-entered the water. "I'll take the far side, you stay on this side. That way, we won't have four horses stirring up the bottom in a line. This grey/green water won't show much, but we'll go upstream maybe a half-mile before we get out."

"Lead the way, my friend. I'm just a'followin' along as you say," answered Ezra, watching Gabriel gig Ebony into the water. The lead line to the sorrel packhorse stretched tight as the mare balked a little but was tugged forward and followed the stallion. Once across, Gabriel looked back to see Ezra stepping his bay off the bank, the chestnut packhorse willingly following. With Gabriel on the west edge and Ezra on the east edge of the river, they walked their mounts in water that touched the bottoms of their stirrups. The gravelly bottom made the going easy, and the murky water showed little.

Gabriel was eyeing the upstream area, looking for a low bank to make climbing out easy, when Ezra shouted and the big bay snorted, rearing up and pawing at the water. Ezra grabbed his saddle pistol with one hand to hold tight to the reins with the other, clasping the sides of the horse with his legs and searching the water for what was frightening his horse. He lowered the pistol, quickly took aim, and fired at the water near a low-hanging limb from an elm tree. He cocked the hammer on the second barrel and fired again. Quickly jamming the pistol back into the holster, he jerked the reins of the bay to move into the middle of the stream. With several glances over his shoulder toward the tree and the nearby water, he slapped his legs to the bay, pulled the lead line that was wrapped around the saddle horn taut, and mounted the bank in front of an astounded Gabriel.

Gabriel reined Ebony out of the water, and once atop the bank, stepped down near Ezra, who was stroking his horse's neck, trying to calm the shaking and prancing horse. Gabriel asked, "What was that all about?"

"Cottonmouth! Big 'un!" declared Ezra, still working to settle the bay down.

"Oh, is that all?" stated Gabriel.

"Is that all? If that'd been you, you'da jumped clear to this bank from your saddle! I know you an' snakes, and there ain't been a time you wanted to be in the same country as one, much less have one swimming directly at you!"

Gabriel laughed, "You're right about that, my friend, but let's push on. I wanna reach the next river that Wing told me about, and he said it's about a day or less from here. There's supposed to be more hills and such that would be good cover for whatever we decide."

"Suits me, long as there ain't no cottonmouth snakes!" grumbled Ezra, climbing back aboard and following Gabriel.

25 / Mesa

The sun searched for a resting place on the western horizon as Gabriel and Ezra crossed the Fall River. They worked through the bare hickory and oak trees to climb the slope to the flat-topped mesa that stood overlooking the wide prairie they had crossed. Once atop, they picked a campsite at the edge of a thick grouping of hickory, hobbled the horses, and laid out the gear for the camp. Gabriel reached into the bottom of his saddlebags and withdrew a leather case that held the Dollond brass telescope that had been the pride of his father's collection. Made in London, the telescope had four barrels of brass that collapsed to ten inches and expanded to forty inches. "I'm gonna take a look at our backtrail, see if there's any sign of those bounty hunters," declared Gabriel as Ezra started preparing the vittles.

With a nod from Ezra, Gabriel walked to the mesa's edge, pushed through the lower brush, and found a pair of boulders perched on the rim. He sat, drew up his knees, and extended the scope for his first survey of the flats. They had purposely ridden directly across the dry land that Gabriel thought might be an ancient lakebed, leaving tracks enough for a greenhorn to follow. The land below the mesa was scarred with multiple feeder creeks that flowed into the Fall River, most being quite small and several carrying water only after a rainfall. But Gabriel thought those same draws would offer shelter for anyone following them, also making them susceptible to attack from the mesa top. The flat-top rose about a hundred fifty feet above the valley floor, giving excellent views of the wide grasslands between them and the distant Verdigris River.

With the sun at his back, he had an excellent panorama before him. Carefully scanning the area for any movement, he spotted several deer moving to the water for their evening drink, a couple coyotes playing in the grass, probably chasing rabbits, and a red-shouldered hawk circling overhead. But no bounty hunters.

His mind was circling the problem of the bounty hunters as he walked back into camp. Ezra had a small fire going, and the coffeepot was doing its dance at the edge of the coals. He looked at his friend, grinned, and said, "I think it'll be a day or two 'fore they catch up with us, but I don't think we could find a better place to hold the meeting than right here."

Ezra nodded past the fire. "With that bald flat out there and the trees lining the rim, we've got good cover from three directions, and the wide-open behind us, so I think you're right."

"Tomorrow I wanna learn everything I can about this mesa and trails up from the bottom. We came up the obvious one, but I'm sure there are others. We need to know the area well and plan out what we wanna do. I don't think these are men that will be easily beaten, they've shown a lot of grit followin' us this far, so they won't give up easy."

"Ummhmm, but we've done in more'n these. Remember those river pirates? There was twice as many of them, and we showed 'em what for," declared Ezra, smacking his fist into his palm.

"Yeah, but we took them by surprise, and we were on the attack. Now the tables are turned; we don't know when, where, or how they're gonna come at us. And before you say it, I agree that we need to do the attacking before they do. But as of right now, we don't even know where they are to attack!" grumbled Gabriel, reaching for the coffee pot.

"Well, one thing I do know, and that's we've got a bit of an advantage with that thing," added Ezra, pointing at the scope on Gabriel's lap.

"Hopefully. But I think they've got themselves a good tracker, and he'll probably be scoutin' out far ahead of the others, so we might need to try to make them think we are where we're not!"

"How we gonna do that?" asked Ezra, sitting forward to pour his coffee.

"That I don't know, at least not yet, but we need to be thinkin' on it."

*   *   *   *   *

The wide trail between the Osage village and Fort Caron-delet allowed the band to travel by twos, side by side. Led by Bucky Ledbetter, the tracker, and Squirrel, the group was scattered along the trail, none showing any enthusiasm for their task. Frenchy looked at Frank, "Well, at least he was right about their being in the village. Now, hopefully we can get a better lead on 'em from the traders."

Frank grunted, "Bucky's been doin' good, an' if they can be found, he'll be fer doin' it."

"We'll need to get some more supplies here, won't we?" asked Frenchy.

"You payin'?" growled Frank.

"I don't have any money!" replied Frenchy.

"If we don't get some supplies, these men ain't gonna go no further! They're already gripin' we been on the hunt too long."

From behind them came a retort, "Three weeks is long 'nuff to hunt for one man!" shouted Aaron Caldwell, the man who was usually silent. "An' what you're sayin' we'll get for bringin' him in is gettin' littler an' littler! We've 'bout got our gullets full o' yore promises!"

"Hear, hear!" answered Edgar Reese, and even Squirrel had turned in his saddle to add his, "That's right!" to the growing complaints.

"Aw, shut up! All o' ya! We'll keep goin' long as I say an' there ain't no quittin', got that?" shouted Frank, twisting in his saddle so everyone could hear.

There was a grumbling among all the men, but no one voiced any more complaints. Frank turned to Frenchy, "You're sure 'bout this bounty? Bein' a thousand dollars, I mean."

"Of course, and I think we can get more outta the old man. Maybe twice as much if we work it right," surmised Frenchy, anxious to placate the bigger Frank.

Frank nodded at the break in the trees, "There's the fort. We'll see what we need to do to get some supplies."

"And find out about Stonecroft!" added Frenchy, receiving a nod and a grunt from Frank.

They were greeted by a man in the doorway of the fort that stood with britches rolled up, sleeves of his faded union suit pushed up, thumbs behind his galluses, and smoke coming from a meerschaum pipe hanging at one side of his mouth. A knit fisherman's cap adorned his head, and heavy whiskers that weren't quite a beard made his features look dirty. He lifted one hand as he said, *"Bon jour!"*

Frenchy responded, *"Bonjour, monsieur!"*

The man smiled, stepped out of the door, and waited for the men to step down. Frenchy spoke, first in French, then in English, to tell him they needed supplies.

"Oui, oui. We have plenty of supplies. Do you have pelts to trade?" asked the man known as Adrien.

"No, no, we'll just pay fer 'em. But we need a good bunch, so as you pick 'em, and we'll load 'em," answered Frank. "First, we need some cornmeal, sugar, salt, flour, beans, an' then some powder and lead. We prob'ly oughta get some trade goods fer them Injuns, don't you think, Frenchy?" growled the big man, looking at his partner.

"Yes, yes. That would be good. We'll be goin' to the Osage and tradin'." He looked at Adrien, "By the way, some friends of ours came through here a few days ago. They're scoutin' things out for us, and we want to make sure we're on the right track. Do you remember a young fella, name of Gabriel Stonecroft, tall and with blond hair? He was with a negra, his helper."

"Why, yes, there were two men like that, and they had an Osage woman with them too. I believe they said they were going on a buffalo hunt with her people. Let's see, now." He paused, thinking, "Yes, I believe he said they might go as far as the Verdigris, the site of the other Chouteau post."

"Good, good," replied Frenchy, nodding at Frank, "That's exactly what we had discussed. He'll probably be waiting for us there. How far would you say it is?"

"About four days, give or take. The wagons take four to five days from here, but since the road improves, maybe less," answered Adrien.

As the men spoke, the clerk fetched the supplies, made a note of them, and watched as the men took them to the packhorses. The counter was empty when he began adding up the tally. He looked at Frank, expecting the big man to be preparing to pay, but he stood leaning on the counter. "That will be twenty-six dollars," declared Adrien, forcing a smile.

Frank nodded, turned his back to the clerk, making as if he were retrieving a money pouch, but when he turned around, he held a pistol before him, cocking the hammer as he smiled. "You can keep the change." He pulled the trigger, and the blast and smoke filled the room. The clerk, grabbing his chest, eyes wide with surprise and fear, crumpled to the floor. Another of the three clerks came running into the room, stopped and stared at the body of his co-worker, and gaped at Frank. The big man held a knife waist-high, blade up, lunged forward, grabbed the clerk by the shirt, and pulled him into the knife. The clerk gasped and grabbed at Frank, then slid to the floor.

Frank and Frenchy heard a shot from outside and looked at the door, expecting the other clerk, but no one appeared. Frank walked to the door, saw Bucky standing over the body of the third trader, and grinning at Frank. The big man nodded his approval, then barked orders, "Let's get those supplies tied down. We've got a ways to go, so mount up!"

Frank spoke to Frenchy, "Let's lock this place down. We can empty it out when we come back through, and maybe get as much for the trade goods as we do for Stonecroft's head!" He turned to the building and stepped through the door, sneered at the dead men, grabbed a hammer and some nails, and went out to nail the door shut. "That'll do for now. Mebbe keep the Injuns out. He looked at Bucky, "Drag that body into the trees!!"

Frenchy spoke low to Frank, "You gonna tell 'em it's four days to the Verdigris?"

"No! They don't need to know. But we better be for findin' them two, or we'll be fightin' our own men," he declared as he swung aboard his mount.

26 / Ploy

They took to the trees, heading opposite directions to scan all the terrain near the mesa. They especially looked for any trails that led to the top or took a distinctive direction away, a trail that would entice tired hunters to take the easy way. Their plan was to learn every probable route that might be taken by the bounty hunters and every possible attack or defensible location nearby. Gabriel thought there was no way to predict what they would do, but if he put himself in their position, maybe he could think it through. By now, some or all of them might be tired of the chase, disgruntled at best, and would be looking for a place to rest up.

They would want to be close to water and graze for the horses, but in a protected area that could be defended in the event of an Indian attack. After all, this was Osage country, and getting mighty close to Kiowa territory. As he worked his way through the trees, he searched for trails and campsites—anything that would offer cover in a running battle.

He needed to know the lay of the land and be able to use it to his advantage, no matter what.

They met up at the base of the steep-sided bluff and Gabriel explained to Ezra what he was thinking. "If we could know where they'll camp, if they choose to camp near here, we'll be a step ahead."

Ezra nodded, "I was thinking the same thing. Follow me," he directed as he reined his bay around. In less than twenty yards, he drew up at the edge of a grass-covered clearing. It bordered the river, offering a low bank and easy access to water, and backed up to the bluff, giving good cover and good access. Gabriel looked around, then stood in his stirrups to look across the river at the flats beyond. Set back and twisted in his seat to look in every direction, then lifted his eyes to the mesa rim. He grinned at Ezra, "Now, if we can just get 'em here, we can formulate a plan."

"What if we made 'em think we camped here?" asked Ezra. "You know, make it look like we came outta the river right to here, had a fire goin'… all the things that make it look like we camped here for a day or more."

Gabriel looked at his friend, let a grin cut his face, and said, "You're pretty good at this deceitful stuff! Let's do it!"

They brought down the packhorses and packs, then picketed all four horses and let them graze at will while they tromped around the area, gathering firewood, making a fire, rolling out bedrolls, and doing everything they could to make it look like they had been there for two or more days. Ezra led the horses to the river to water, moved them around to leave plenty of tracks, took them back to the pickets and repeated the action.

Gabriel looked around, satisfied they were had done their best to make a phony camp, then suggested, "How 'bout you goin' ahead and making a meal for us while I go back up top and use my scope to have a look-see?"

Ezra grinned, pleased with his suggestion and the plan that was beginning to formulate, and replied, "Of course. The longer we stay here, the more it'll look like we've been here a while. As long as we're gone when they come, that is!"

*   *   *   *   *

Crazy Wolf slid his horse to a stop beside Blue Corn's and Eagle's Wing. He twisted around to point behind him, "They come. The white men our scout told of that went to our village. They are this many," he said, holding up all the fingers of one hand and one of the other.

The Osage were on the trail, returning to their village near Fort Carondelet. Travois were loaded with buffalo meat, smoked and fresh, horses were packed heavy and many of the people walked beside the animals. They knew they were not in danger, with more than forty warriors and many women who could shoot both rifle and bow as well as any man, they feared no one. But both Corn and Wing knew these men were on the trail of the men that had hunted with them and who fought against the Pawnee at their side. For these to go against their friends was the same as an attack on them.

Wing looked at Blue Corn and started to speak, but the chief held up his hand, "I know what you would do. Go, and may you and all our warriors return soon."

Wing nodded, reined his mount around, and went among the people, choosing the warriors to accompany him. Honey Bear saw him and asked, "Is it the men that are after White Cougar?"

"Yes."

"Then I will go with you," she declared, laying the rifle given her by Gabriel across the withers of her horse and looking at the war leader. A simple nod from him was all that was needed, and she followed him as he gathered his band. He chose eight other proven warriors to make the complement of his band ten, all blooded fighters and warriors eager to do battle. Most had come to know and respect both Gabriel and Ezra during the skirmish with the Pawnee and on the hunt and considered both men friends. The bond of brotherhood was often stronger than that of blood or race, and these were warriors who had often offered their lives in defense of friends and family. There were no reservations or hesitation on the part of any; eagerness and determination showed on their faces and in their stance.

Eagle's Wing led them into the trees since they did not want to make contact with the white men until the time chosen by Wing, which would be after they knew the whereabouts of their friends. Until that time, they would follow or shadow these men to learn more of their enemy.

*   *   *   *   *

Bucky rode back toward the others at a canter, reined up, and spoke to Frank and Frenchy. "You might wanna take to the trees or sumpin'. That whole village o' Osage is comin' back, and they're ridin' this trail. I don't think they'll wanna move aside for you."

"I ain't gonna move aside for no bunch o' squaws and kids!" declared Frank, indignant that Bucky would even suggest it.

Bucky laughed, "Well, you do what you want. But if'n I was you and had to face about forty warriors, ever' one as tall or taller'n you and all of 'em meaner a bear with a thorn in his paw, I'd skedaddle!" Without another comment, he gigged his horse into a brushy draw that had grey cottonwoods along the bank.

Frenchy looked at Frank, then peered down the trail, and although he saw nothing, he reined his horse after Bucky. When the other three, including the ever-faithful friend of Frank, Squirrel, kicked their horses into the trees, Frank grumbled and grudgingly followed.

They found a dim game trail that took them deeper into the trees and near the top of a low mound that gave a dim view of the trail below. Less than a quarter of an hour later, the first of the village showed. Evidently one of the leaders was at the head of the line; he rode tall and was accompanied by another man who rode with dignity. Both had feathers in their scalp locks and a blanket loosely around one shoulder and draped over their legs. It was a cool morning, and others wore buffalo robes, blankets, or capotes. The white men had stepped to the ground and stayed still, but craned to see as much as possible from their obscure perch. The procession had many loaded horses and several heavily laden travois. The bounty of the hunt was evident, not just in the bundles of meat, but also in the jovial mood of the people. The long line was interspersed with warriors, showing lances and other weapons always at the ready and their vigilance evident by their manner and carriage.

Bucky stepped up beside Frank, nudged him, and whispered, "See what I mean? Those are the biggest Injuns I ever did see!"

"Yeah, I see what'chu mean. And these are the ones that put their enemies' heads on a stick?"

"Yup, they's the ones, all right."

"Did you see any sign of the two we're lookin' for?" asked Frenchy.

"Nah, I don't think they're with 'em, but I been watchin' for 'em," answered Bucky.

"When we come back, is there any way we won't cross them?" asked Frank, showing his growing fear of the Osage warriors.

"Oh, I b'lieve I can find a way. I don't hanker to tangle with 'em, no sir," answered Bucky, "But what about all that stuff at the trader's fort?"

"Hummm, yeah. We'll have to give it some thought, I reckon." He lifted his eyes to the sky to judge the remaining daylight, "Reckon we can make it to the site of the buffalo hunt 'fore dark?"

Bucky also looked at the sky, judged it to be mid-after-noon, and answered, "Mebbe, if we push it. Ain't too far, maybe ten, twelve mile. There's a good campsite this side of it, so we could probably make it."

"Good, then let's get a move on," declared Frank, trying to regain his bluster.

They had been pushing hard for three days since leaving the fort and seemed to be no nearer their prey than before. Frank and Frenchy had talked about the resentful men and agreed they couldn't push them much further without some indication they were getting close to their quarry. Frank was thinking the men wouldn't be far from the hunting grounds, having no reason to push themselves.

He was certain that Stonecroft had no idea they were fol-lowing, and he planned to catch them unaware and take them without a fight. At the thought, he remembered the last time he'd tangled with the man and rubbed his arm, which still hurt from the break but was healing well. He thought about what he'd like to do to the lanky young man who had shamed him in front of his men. But that would have to wait; there was a little matter of money, and the more he talked with Frenchy, the more certain he was that the man hadn't told him everything about the bounty. He thought he might be trying to hold out on them, and if so, that meant the bounty could be considerably more than any thousand dollars. He grinned at the thought of that much money in hand and what he could do with it, especially if he didn't have to share it.

27 / Brigands

The setting sun was bright in their eyes as it painted the western sky with its brilliant gold and orange. The silhouette of a mounted man stood crosswise in the trail, easily recognizable by his tattered hat and the way he slouched in his saddle. With hands stacked on the pommel, he waited for the men to come near. When Frank and Frenchy reined up beside him, Bucky pointed to the timber-covered bluff, "That was the Injun camp, and they had their hunt just t'other side. Grounds all tore up by them buffler, an' the ones we're huntin' pulled out an' went thataway," pointing to the south end of the bluff toward the setting sun. "I can recognize the tracks o' that big black anywhere!"

"So, they went acrost the buffler' trail?" asked Frank.

"Yup," answered the tracker.

"Can you foller their sign?" grumbled Frank, squirming in his hard saddle.

"Ummhmm, but not till mornin'," declared Bucky.

"How far behind 'em are we?" asked Frenchy.

"Oh, day, day n' a half. They ain't movin' fast, so we could push it an' crowd 'em a little," answered Bucky.

The pack made their camp near the same stream used by the Osage, all the disgruntled men grumbling and griping, but none loud enough to raise the ire of Frank, who grumbled enough himself. He was kicking at his bedroll, trying to roll it out under a big oak when Squirrel came to his side and asked, "How much longer we gonna chase these two?"

Frank turned on his longtime sidekick and snarled, "Till we catch 'em, what'chu think?"

"All them others," nodding at the other men, "ain't happy. Not me, mind you, just them. They's wantin' to get back to the river and go back to piratin'."

"Piratin? You mean they wants to get back on the river? One thing they ain't thinkin' 'bout—we ain't got no boat!" growled Frank, dropping to his knees to straighten his blankets. He stood facing Squirrel, "Bucky said we ain't more'n a day'n a half from catchin' up to them two." He lowered his voice and drew Squirrel near, "We can get 'em, an' then we can get rid o' the complainers on our way back," grinning.

Squirrel smiled and laughed, "Can I use muh knife?" He delighted in sneak attacks on sleeping quarry, slitting their throats while they slept. He had often exacted his vengeance on bigger foes who had taunted him for his small stature and squeaky voice. Now with the thought of doing in some of those he traveled with, most having goaded him at one time or another, gave him a certain glee that was readily understood by Frank.

Frank slapped him on the back, "Course you can, my friend, course you can!"

Bucky had taken a nice sized whitetail doe that now hung from the big branch of a nearby oak. Frenchy had been tasked with the cooking and had cut the backstraps and sliced them into several palm-sized steaks that now sizzled over the fire. Well-supplied after their raid on the traders, a pot of water was bouncing at the edge, and Frenchy lifted the lid to drop in a handful of fresh ground coffee. He had made a pan full of biscuits that now baked beside the fire under a pile of hot coal resting on the lid, some yampa root gathered by Bucky had been pushed under the coals at the edge of the fire and Frenchy sat back to watch.

The others had finished their chores, tending the horses, stacking the gear, and rolling out the bedrolls, and came to the fire one at a time, anxious for the evening meal. They sat quiet, waiting and staring at the flames, until Edgar Reese asked, "So, how much longer?" The question was asked of the fire without Reese looking at anyone in particular.

Frank glared at the man and answered, "Bucky says we're a day, day'n a half behind 'em. He said they ain't in no hurry, ain't movin' fast, so if we get a early start in the mornin', we might catch up to 'em by nightfall, or mebbe a little later."

Edgar looked at Frank, was quiet for a moment before he answered. Edgar knew Frank to be a mean man and dirty fighter, thinking nothing of shooting a man in the back or worse, but he also knew his own skills of fighting and thought he could best Frank in a stand-up fight. Frank wasn't one to do anything fair, though. He fought to win, no matter what it took. Edgar looked at the big man and answered, "Two days, then. Two days. If we ain't got 'em by then, I'm pullin' out!"

Frank glared at Edgar and growled, "Mighty hard to ride out when you're weighed down with lead!"

"That goes two ways, Frank," answered Edgar, meeting Frank's stare with his own.

Frenchy interjected, "Food's ready! Let's eat!"

For an awkward moment, no one moved until Frank dropped his eyes and snatched up a plate, "Put some meat on there!" he demanded, pointing to the tin plate. He stood and kicked the coals from atop the pan of biscuits and stabbed one with his knife, then rooted around in the coals at the edge of the fire and stabbed a couple yampa roots and put them on his plate. He poured himself a cup of coffee and went off by himself to sulk in the dark at the edge of the light.

Frank had the grumbling bunch on the trail by first light. Bucky had left a few minutes earlier, knowing the basic direction taken by their quarry, and pushed his horse onto the churned-up soil of the buffalo trail. An experienced tracker can tell the age of a track by the weathering and drying of the sign. Bucky found it easier to follow the trail of Gabriel and Ezra than expected, with the tracks left by their horses distinct from the trail of the buffalo, not only in size and shape but in freshness. The buffalo turned soil had dried and crumbled, while the tracks of the horses were darker, fresher, and followed a more direct route. Bucky kicked his horse to a canter, pushing to gain on the two men.

After less than an hour traveling in the path of the bison, Bucky spotted where his prey had turned to the west and was immediately on the trail. He topped out on a slight knoll to search the distance for the possible objective of the two men. He stood, the rein of his mount in one hand, the other shielding his eyes, as he stared to the west toward the Verdigris River. The tree-lined bank gave evidence of the river's course and Bucky smiled, seeing the obvious tracks of the four horses he was pursuing. He mounted up and rode from the knoll, choosing to vary his route, not directly following the tracks of the two men. If they were watching their back-trail as he suspected, he didn't want to give himself away, so he stayed in the low swales and dry gullies of the land.

Bucky stopped often to leave sign on the trail to make it easier for Frank and the others to follow, sometimes with rocks or sticks making an arrow on the ground, or a blaze on trees or branches broken and twisted to point the way. He knew he had to make it simple with Frank and his men lacking even basic woodsman skills.

When he came to the Verdigris, he rode the east bank, searching for the sign of where the two men crossed or made camp. Within a few moments, he found their camp, and stood on the bank, to see if he could determine where they'd crossed the river and rose up on the far bank. Almost directly across from the camp, he saw the obvious signs of the four horses crossing the sandbar and moving up to the grass on the far side. He grinned, believing Gabriel and Ezra did not know they were being followed and had made no effort to obscure their trail. He chuckled and shook his head as he thought, "This is almost too easy! They won't know what hit 'em when we catch up to 'em, probably tomorrow."

Bucky stripped the gear from his horse and picketed him on some grass, then stretched out under the big oak to catch up on some sleep while he waited for Frank and his bunch of cutthroats. He smiled as he drifted off to sleep, thinking about what he would do with his share of the bounty money.

When Frank and the others rode up, Bucky stood, hands on his hips, grinning. Frank growled, "I thought you said we'd find 'em by now."

"They ain't far, an' they ain't movin' fast, so I'm sure they don't know we're followin' 'em." He turned and pointed to the far bank, "See there? That's where they crossed over an' they made their camp here. Those tracks ain't that old so, I know we'll catch up to 'em tomorrow!" Bucky turned back to face Frank, a satisfied smirk on his face. He looked at the others, "So, men, I think we'll be spendin' our money from that reward mighty soon! An' I got me a girl back in New Madrid that's just pinin' for my return!"

Edgar and Aaron, sitting their horses behind Frank and Frenchy, looked at one another, "Bout time!" growled Edgar, to the nodding agreement of Aaron. The two had buddied up and rode together, making Frank think they were planning their getaway or some other subterfuge. As is the way of thieves and other criminals, no one trusts the other, always judging them by their own ways and thoughts. But that is the way of people in general; the measure used to judge others is the one we know best, and that is ourselves. Others are taller or shorter than we are, bigger or skinnier, meaner or better. And in the eyes of those whose lives are spent deceiving and taking advantage of others, they assume everyone is as deceptive and crooked as they are and are unable to trust anyone. Frank's only way of dealing with those who turned on him was to turn on them first, and he had already started forming his alliances and plans to achieve his ends.

28 / Chase

When Frank pushed to his elbows, the first light of morning had already blushed pink and faded. He groaned as he rose, angry at the new day and his poor sleep of the night before. No one had started the fire, and a quick glance told him Bucky was gone. He growled, "Get up! Now!" barking at no one and everyone. He rolled his blankets and staggered to where the horses were picketed. Grabbing his saddle and bridle, he snatched at the lead rope of his horse, who jerked back wide-eyed, having experienced the anger of the man before. Frank growled, "C'mere, you crowbait!" and forcibly pulled the grey horse close. Keeping one hand on the lead, he swung the blanket, then the saddle onto the horse's back, and with the animal settled down, began wrapping and binding the girth.

The others had followed his lead, grumbling all the way. Edgar asked, "Ain't we gonna eat? Have some coffee at least?"

"No, you slept too long. We gotta move out!" As he

snarled, he caught some movement and looked across the river to see Bucky returning already. He walked to the edge of the bank and hollered, "Find 'em already?"

"No! They wiped out their tracks, so I'm gonna have to search a mite to find 'em. Anybody over there up an' at 'em to give me a hand?" hollered Bucky, standing in his stirrups and cupping his hands to his mouth.

"I will, hold on!" answered Frank, and mumbling as he turned, he looked at Edgar, "You an' Aaron put on some coffee an' heat up them biscuits an' meat. We'll be back soon for some."

Edgar grinned, relieved, and answered, "Sure, boss, I'll do that!"

Frank mounted and started to the river but was stopped by Bucky, who shouted from the other side, "You ride the bank on that side and see if they cross back. I'll do the same o'er here!"

Frank waved an acknowledgment and reined his horse along the bank to start searching. He had ridden about a hundred yards, in and out of the trees, searching the riverbank, sandbars, and tree line for any sign, when he saw what he thought might be their tracks. He stepped down and searched the deep leaves and branches, then grabbed a stick and used it to stir up the leaves. He followed the faint trail, came to a stretch with dried grass and nothing much else, and saw the distinct tracks of at least two horses. He looked ahead, saw the trail leading back to the riverbank where the stream had bent back on itself, and mounted up.

Returning to the bank across from Bucky, he stood in his stirrups and hollered, "Think I found somethin'!" and waved him over. They followed the tracks across the neck of land between the bends in the river and came to the bank, where the tracks went into the water. Bucky reined up, shaded his eyes to look across the river, "They went in, but I can't see where they came out!" Frank was also looking, and the far bank kept its secret of anyone crossing.

"Now what?" growled Frank, looking at his tracker.

Bucky looked at the big man, pulled out his corncob pipe and lit the remains of the tobacco. After drawing a deep puff, he answered, "Same as what we just did. You take this bank, I'll cross over," and gigged his horse into the water. Both men rode through the thickening trees, weaving in and out, searching the deep leaves and grasses, looking for any sign that would tell of the passing of two men and four horses. After another quarter-hour, Bucky hollered, "Found 'em!" Frank reined back into the trees and neared the bank. He saw Bucky waving from the far shore, and hollering, "I'll follow 'em, you come on with the others!" Frank waved and turned back to the camp. He was as anxious for some food and coffee as he was for the pursuit.

The long stretch of flatlands between the Verdigris and Fall Rivers offered little respite to the men who now had more to complain about. The cold winter wind tore at their clothing, wrapping icy fingers around their throats and reaching into their tattered clothes. Squirrel was the first to grab his blankets and wrap them around him. The others followed his lead and soon their horses, heads hanging, icicles dangling from their manes and noses, each footfall breaking ice that clung to long, dry grasses, began to stagger and stumble. Frank's horse went to his knees, launching the burly man over his head to roll in the jumble of icicles. The cold wind was merciless and bit at any exposed flesh.

Frenchy hollered, "We gotta stop and have a fire! We're killin' these horses!"

Edgar growled, "Killin' ourselves, ya mean."

Frank had scrambled to his feet and held the reins of his horse in his hand as he looked for any shelter. He spotted some brush and treetops protruding from a low swale and pointed, "There!" He started walking toward the promised cover. There was a shallow pool of water in the bottom, but the trees and slope of the land gave a break from the icy wind and the men readily stepped down, letting their horses drink from the ice-rimmed pool. Aaron had gathered an armload of wood, and Edgar and Squirrel fetched some kindling and soon had a fire blazing. The men stood around the flames, holding their hands out and rubbing them together to get the blood flowing again. The crusted ice on their coats dripped into small puddles at their feet and the men stood quiet, listening to the eerie wind whistle through the skeletal branches of the trees above their heads.

Bucky found their retreat and rode down into the low shelter. He stepped down and walked to the fire, joining the men by the flames. He looked at Frank, "There's a better campsite a little ways further. It's acrost the river, but up against a bluff, protected by the trees, lotsa grass. Be a good place to wait out this storm, which prob'ly won't last long. Them fellas camped there and left it today. Weren't gone but a couple hours when I came onto the camp." He paused, looking around, "And with this storm, they might even turn around and come back to it and find us there!"

The others looked around at one another, and Frank asked, "How far?"

"Oh, a mile or two, tha's all," answered the grinning tracker.

"We'll get warm, give the horses a breather, then we'll head out. Mebbe the wind'll let up a mite," declared Frank, thinking of his own comfort more than the others.

★   ★   ★   ★   ★

Gabriel and Ezra had moved back to the top of the mesa and found a better camp than before. A large rise of rock offered a cove of cover, with an overhang and back cover. They had a warm fire within the small enclave, and their horses were tethered at the far end of the rocks, enjoying the cover from the cold wind. The misty rain that quickly turned to ice had let up, but the wind continued to howl and whine around the rocks. The fire was safe from discovery, with the surrounding rocks shielding it from view and the wind. Gabriel had set up a long flat stone as a reflector to keep most of the heat within the cove.

The sun hid in shame, failing to give the light and warmth that was its job, and took refuge behind the tall dark grey clouds that waltzed across the sky. The semi-darkness fore-told of the coming night, and the two friends watched the coffee pot do its dance as they awaited the daily brew.

"Ya think they'll come tonight?" asked Ezra, getting tired of the waiting game. He was anxious to put an end to this cat and mouse nonsense, especially when he thought of himself as the mouse.

"Dunno. Depends on how close they are. If their scout finds the camp below, then maybe. But I'll take a look soon. The rain's let up, but that wind still cuts. I'll take a good look-see soon. If they do, this ice might make sneakin' around a little precarious."

"Aw, not much. I don't think the leaves got too icy. Prob'ly just wet, and that'll make it quieter."

"Maybe," answered Gabriel, thinking.

The wind became intermittent, whispering through the trees and around the rocks, saying its goodbyes for the com-ing night. Gabriel tucked the telescope case into his shirt, slipped on the heavy coat, and started for the rocks at the edge of the mesa. He had no sooner taken his seat and begun to lift his scope than he saw movement in the open flats be-yond. He brought up his knees for support and laid the scope out, then brought the eyepiece up and put the cold brass against his face, focused the lens, and scanned the terrain. There—several men on horseback, trotting their mounts as they headed straight toward the bluff. He hunkered down against the cold, held the long scope steady, and focused on the lead riders.

All of the men were bundled, chins in their collars, hats pulled down, but judging by size only, the lead man was his nemesis from New Madrid. Six men total, no others the size of their leader, and one considerably smaller, wiry looking. Gabriel remembered the little skinny runt who'd sided the big man when he was fighting and thought he had been called Rabbit or Squirrel. That's it...Squirrel. Gabriel was now certain these were the same ones who had confronted them in New Madrid, but now there were more. There had been only four at the inn, but now six men followed. Perhaps the others were the reason for the pursuit. Maybe they had brought the news of the bounty. No matter. Gabriel felt a fight was coming, and he was determined this would be a fight to finish any more pursuit. He knew Ezra would agree since they were tired of running and would run no more.

29 / Sabotage

Gabriel gave the shrill repeated cry of the nighthawk to summon Ezra to his side. His friend came quickly and quietly, kneeling on the rock behind Gabriel. Gabe whispered as he kept his eye to the scope, "They're coming. It is the bunch from New Madrid; I recognized the mousy one as well as the big one. Not sure 'bout the rest, but they're definitely on our trail." He handed the scope back to Ezra to take a look. As he stared down the tube, Gabe said, "Looks like they're headed straight to the camp. Their scout musta found it like we hoped."

"You're right. What'chu think we should do?" asked Ezra, lowering the scope to look at his friend.

"Let 'em get settled in, an' we'll get closer. Listen in on 'em and see if we can make out their plans, then decide."

The bounty hunters settled into their camp, glad to escape the cold winter wind and have a warm fire and hot meal.

More focused on their comfort than their predicament, the grumbling had subsided, howbeit temporarily. Frenchy had more or less inherited the job of cooking, while the others were tasked with taking care of the horses and gear. With more venison strips hanging over the fire, a pot of beans dangling over the flames, and johnnycakes in the pan, the men stared at the flames and anticipated the good meal.

Edgar looked at Bucky, "So, those two left this camp today?"

"Yup, no more'n a couple hours 'fore I got here. What with the wind and ice, don't think they went too far, prob'ly found shelter along the trail and ducked their heads instead o' comin' back. We'll find 'em in the mornin'," he declared, confidently.

When Frenchy pronounced the meal ready, they set to, and with full plates and cups, they eagerly did their best to clean plates and pots of everything edible. When they sat back to enjoy full bellies and warm feet, Frank surprised them when he brought out a jug and passed the whiskey around.

"Now, that's more like it!" proclaimed Aaron, usually one to keep his silence. He took a long draught and passed the jug to Edgar. His friend put his finger through the loop and rested the jug on his bent elbow, putting the mouth to his lips and chugging a long drink. His action raised the protests of the others, hoping there would be plenty for all and fearing the oft complaining drinker would leave little for the others. But they were not disappointed when Frank assured them, "There's plenty for ever'body, just sit easy."

Gabriel and Ezra split up, with Gabe taking the longer route of approaching the camp from the downstream edge of the river, while Ezra dropped from the mesa's ridge toward the north tree line. The plan was to listen in, wait for them to turn in, and do what damage they could without endangering themselves. The real attack wouldn't happen until first light.

Ezra chose each step, listening to the crunch of the thin layers of ice from the day's storm. But the night winds had brought a warmth that began to melt the icicles that hung from the bare branches of the elm, hickory, and oak trees. The intermittent wind came in gusts, each causing a rattle within the woods as ice fell to the ground, giving the sound of hundreds of wood nymphs dancing through the forest. But it covered the approach of the two friends who paced their movements with the gusts.

The night was full dark, but the clouds of the storm had passed. Stars signaled their presence with blinking lanterns, and the moon was waxing toward full. With eyes now accustomed to the darkness, both Ezra and Gabriel moved confidently toward the camp. Ezra was on elbows and knees, pistol in hand, and as he got within earshot of the camp, he dropped silently to his belly to listen.

Gabriel made good time, further from the camp when he descended from the mesa, he trotted through the damp woods until he came to the riverbank. Using both the sounds of the wind and the melting ice, and the chuckle of the river, he approached the camp, slowly moving from tree to tree.

When he was within about twenty feet, he lowered himself to one knee. With one of the saddle pistols in his hand and the other in his belt, he waited and watched. The glow of the campfire added to the light of the night, allowing Gabe to recognize all four of the men from New Madrid.

While the others worked on the jug, Frenchy gave a slight nod to Frank for the two of them to step aside and talk. As Frank came to his side, Frenchy asked, "You think Bucky is right about catching up with those two tomorrow?"

"No reason not to think that. He's as hungry for a fight as the rest of us, if not more," answered the big man.

"Then, if we get them, are all of us heading back right away?" asked Frenchy, watching Frank's reaction to be sure he understood what was implied.

Frank chuckled, dropped his head and looked at the ground grinning, "Oh, there's probably two or three that might be left behind."

Frenchy grinned, nodding his head, "Just don't forget, you need me to know where to get the reward, and I need you to get the job done. That bounty will be a bit bigger if its only shared two ways instead of six."

"Oh, I ain't forgettin' nothin'. Especially the part about gettin' more'n the original thousand dollars!"

Frenchy looked at Frank, determined to keep the increased amount of the bounty to himself, making him think he was the only one that could get the additional money. He needed that extra incentive for his own protection. He didn't trust Frank any more than Frank trusted him. "Oh, we'll get it all right. I have no doubts about that, but there were conditions put on that extra thousand, so keep that in mind as you keep me healthy."

Frank growled as he started back to the fire, hoping to get another slug of the whiskey before it was all gone.

Ezra saw the big man and another walk away from the fire as the rest of the men passed the jug around. His position gave him a good view of those at the fire, and he observed and listened as they watched the other two go off by themselves. The man with the jug looked at the retreating pair, then the others and started to lift the jug but spoke quietly, "Wonder what they're up to?" and tipped the jug for another snort.

"Whatchu mean?" asked the man beside him.

Edgar said, "Them two," nodding toward Frank and Frenchy, "like they's plannin' somethin' that don't include us! I don't like it!"

Aaron looked at the dark figures away from the fire, "Yeah, an' I don't trust Frank. He'd as soon shoot us as share with us."

Squirrel piped in, "Frank wouldn't do that!"

"Maybe not to you, since you're his lap dog. But all of us have seen Frank turn on others before. I'm just sayin' we need to watch each other's back!" answered Edgar, passing the jug to Aaron.

Squirrel took the jug from Aaron and tipped it up, thinking about his agreement with Frank and what he was going to do with his knife. When he dropped the jug from his lips, he smiled in anticipation of his appointed task.

Little more was said among the men as they went to their blankets, turning in for the night. Ezra and Gabriel watched and waited, giving ample time for the men to drop into a sound sleep. Surprisingly, they did not post a guard. Although their scout was woods-wise, and all knew they were in Indian country, they felt themselves safe enough in their camp, and no one wanted to be the one to miss out on sleep by being the lookout. Besides, if anyone was to attack, they were more than capable of defending themselves, or so they thought. Such is the man who thinks he is stronger, smarter, and craftier than anyone else. It's an arrogance that runs in the mind of those who think themselves beyond the reach of law or retribution, leaving them free to exert their will on anyone they believed to be weaker.

Edgar and Aaron lay feet to the fire on the south side, closest to Gabriel. Frank, Squirrel, and Frenchy were close to one another on the opposite side, and Bucky was off by himself nearer the tree line at the bottom of the steep slope of the mesa. Gabriel had already judged the loner to be more savvy than the others and the one to be wary of, while the two nearest him were the most careless. He and Ezra had agreed that if possible, they would try to disarm some of the men if it could be done secretly.

Giving the men a good hour after turning in, Gabriel listened to the night sounds, not just of the occasional nighthawk or the great horned owl or the chirping call of the mockingbird, but the snorts, coughs, and snores of the men. Most were breathing the regular rhythm of sleep as Gabriel began his belly-down approach toward the two men. He moved slowly and stealthily, taking his time and remaining ever watchful. He lifted one arm and the opposite leg, raising his body from the ground to prevent the shuffling sound of leather sliding on the ground, which was a dead giveaway. His slow, methodical movement brought him close to the heads of the two men, whose rifles were lying nearby, barrels resting behind the cantles of the saddles they used for pillows.

He waited, letting his breathing slow, heard a bullfrog in the cattails by the river, and then reached toward the rifle nearest the man called Edgar. The sleeping figure was snoring, lips flapping with each exhale, his face toward his friend Aaron. Gabriel reached down, feeling for the jaw screw atop the hammer. He grasped the round knob of the screw and twisted, it turned, hard at first then a little easier. He cupped his hand next to the hammer and felt the flint fall from the jaws. He totally unscrewed the jaw screw and put the top jaw and screw in his pocket. He started to move back when movement across the coals of the fire caught his eye. Bucky had risen from his blankets and with rifle in hand, he quietly moved to the trees in the direction of Ezra to relieve himself.

Gabriel held his breath as he watched the man leave. He had planned to disable the rifle of the man next to Edgar, but with Bucky moving around, he carefully moved back from the sleeping pair, turned, and at a low crouch, went to the trees. Once within cover, he stood, turning back to look. He waited a couple of minutes until Bucky returned from the trees and went to his blankets. When he had settled in, Gabriel moved away, headed for their camp. He and Ezra would plan their next move and prepare themselves for the fight.

30 / Clash

"Just as I started movin' in, that guy got up and came so close he almost stepped on me! After that, well, I just figgered it'd be too risky," explained Ezra as the two friends rekindled their fire to warm up the coffee.

"The way they're lyin' around the fire, I think if we just went back 'bout where we were and wait, as soon as they start to stir, we'll have the drop on 'em, and we take 'em."

"What're we gonna do if they just give up? We can't shoot 'em then," added Ezra.

"I reckon we just disarm 'em and send 'em back to New Madrid," suggested Gabe.

"Oh yeah, I can see 'em just sayin' 'sure Mr. Stonecroft, don't hurt us Mr. Stonecroft. We'll go peaceable and never come back, Mr. Stonecroft!'" mocked Ezra.

Gabriel grinned, shaking his head, and reached for the coffee pot. They both were tense and needed the relief. Neither man expected the bounty hunters to give up without a fight, but they knew they couldn't just charge into their camp shooting—although he had thought about it. As he considered the men below them, he realized he was visually picking targets. Who he would shoot first, and the next. These men were hunting him like an animal and probably had no thought of taking him alive. Remembering the man he killed in the duel, Jason Wilson, and his father, both known to be bloody men that thought little of taking another's life. Any bounty he offered for Gabriel would have no stipulations as to alive or dead. He knew he had to be doubly careful, for these men probably wanted him dead, thinking only of the money they would gain by his death.

He sat back, deep in thought as he mindlessly sipped the hot coffee. Ezra saw the glazed eyes and knew better than to interrupt his thinking, letting his calculating mind work out the problems of their siege. He too sat back, enjoying his coffee and looking at the stars. While most would stare at the flames or flickering coals, they knew they had to preserve their night vision and shield their eyes from the brightness of the fire. The clouds had cleared, and the Milky Way arched overhead. The moon, waxing to full, hung suspended upon nothing, sharing its light with the nocturnal world.

Somewhere a lonesome coyote lifted his cry to the stars, hoping for an answer from another. Below the mesa in the backwater of the river, a bullfrog bragged he was bigger than any other, and a skinny branch held the big-eyed owl who asked his question of the night. Usually, these were comforting sounds, but tonight it reminded Ezra that even if he was to be killed in the looming fight, the frog, owl, and coyote, would sing their night song the next night without him to hear their carol. He was reminded of his father's sermon called *Little Time* taken from James that says, *"For what is your life? It is even a vapor that appeareth for a little time, and then vanish away."* He shook his head and mumbled, "Ain't that the truth?"

"What? What'd you say?" asked Gabriel, roused from his reverie.

Ezra looked up, not realizing he had spoken out loud and answered, "Oh, nothin'. Just rememberin' something my father preached, 'bout life being a vapor."

"Oh," replied Gabriel, sitting forward on his seat. He put his elbows on his knees and leaned forward, looking at Ezra. "I don't think we have much choice. We'll have to take 'em from two sides and do our best. You have your double-barreled saddle pistol and your belt pistol, and I have my three pistols, and with our rifles, we should have more'n enough for six men. You can miss once and I can miss two or three times, and we'll still have enough lead for all of 'em."

"Don't go talkin' 'bout missin'. But I'm takin' my war club anyway!"

"I think the saltiest one of the bunch is that one who got up and went to the trees. After him, it'd be the big one I fought, Frank. But that little one's cagey and as slippery as a snake, so don't underestimate him," said Gabe, reflecting on his evaluation of the men.

"I'd hafta agree with you. But that other'n that went with

Frank and had their little conversation away from the others, he might be capable," added Ezra.

Gabriel looked at the sky, guessing it to be about two to three hours past midnight. He looked at Ezra, "Guess we better get ready."

They quietly checked the loads in each weapon, Ezra choosing to pull the lead from his belt pistol and clean and reload it. The other weapons showed themselves to be ready, and the friends stood, clasped hands, and pulled one another close. Gabe spoke first, "Keep your head down, and don't take any unnecessary chances."

"I'm not the one who takes chances. That honor falls on your shoulders, my friend, so you keep your head down and don't take any chances," replied Ezra.

They separated and walked into the trees, using the shadows of the forest to their advantage, carefully moving from tree to tree and taking a different route than used before. They had developed the practice years before of never repeating themselves in any tactic or movement. Gabe's father had often admonished his son, "Never develop a habit that can be used against you."

When Gabe stepped into place behind the big oak, he watched across the camp for any sign of Ezra. Within moments, he saw nothing more than the end of the barrel of the Lancaster rifle, and he knew Ezra was ready. He glanced over his right shoulder to see the first hint of the dull grey of early morning, and knew that any moment, the sleeping men would arouse.

It was Bucky who stirred first. He looked around the camp, then at the horses, and saw no indication of alarm. Most were standing hipshot, heads hanging, and asleep. He slowly pushed back the blankets, stood with rifle in both hands and searched the surrounding trees for any movement. Seeing none, he stepped near Frank as he started to the woods, but Frank growled, "Where you goin'?"

"Never you mind, Frank. A man's got things to do you don't talk about," answered Bucky abruptly. Without hesitating for a step, he continued to the trees. Gabe was concerned he might see Ezra, but an alarm now would set the others off, and they would have less control. He waited, watching.

Frank stretched, threw his blankets aside, and kicked at Squirrel, "Get up! Get the fire goin'," he ordered, speaking loud enough to wake the others. Gabe took a deep breath and watched as the others started stirring. Squirrel stood and went to the smoldering coals and got down on hands and knees to get the fire going, breaking up the kindling and blowing on the coals. The two men nearest Gabe stirred, sat up, and began to stand. Frenchy was standing then started to follow the path taken by Bucky to the woods, and Gabe saw Bucky returning. So far, the only one with a weapon in hand was Bucky.

Gabe lifted his rifle so only the barrel showed beside the tree and shouted, "Don't move!" His rifle was trained on Bucky, but he watched the others as well. No one moved, then Bucky lunged forward, falling to his stomach and brought his rifle up. Gabe followed him with his front sight and squeezed off his shot. The big Ferguson blasted, bucked, and blew smoke and fire, sending the .65 caliber ball on its prescribed path. Gabe saw the rifle in the hands of Bucky spit fire and smoke and the ball from his rifle dug a trench through the bark of the oak before the disfigured ball tore a hole in Gabe's side, spinning him on his heel. He caught himself and dragged the saddle pistol from his belt, cocking both hammers as he did and swung the barrels toward the two before him, who were grabbing up their rifles. He fired the first barrel just as he heard the bark of Ezra's rifle from beyond the camp.

Gabe saw Edgar grab his belly, lift his eyes to glare at Gabe, and crumple to his knees, blood coming from his mouth and flowing over his hands as he fell. Gabe swung the pistol toward Aaron, who was bringing his rifle up, and squeezed off the second shot. The pistol bucked in his hand and spat smoke that obscured his view of the man, but he heard the rifle roar and saw flame through the smoke. But Aaron had taken the bullet from Gabe's pistol, and his rifle was falling when it discharged into the ground.

Gabe dropped the pistol beside his rifle, dragged his second pistol from his blood-soaked waist, and searched for the other men. With only one shot coming from Ezra, that meant there were at least two, if not three others still standing. He took one step from behind the tree, heard movement to the side, and started to turn but was smacked in the side of the head with something that felt like a sledgehammer. He stumbled to the side and tried to lift his pistol, but it was too heavy. He lifted a hand to his head, brought it down, and saw his hand totally covered with blood. He staggered, his legs felt weak, and he dropped to his knees. His vision narrowed and grew blurry. He heard someone far away shouting, "I got him! I got him!" and he fell forward on his face. The leaves were wet and cold, a rock was under his ribs, he struggled to breathe, and his vision grew dark. He thought, *I must be dying. It's dark. No!* Then he was still.

They came from the trees, covered with black and looking like shadows come alive. All around the circle of the camp, they came closer and closer. Suddenly screams filled the woods, and Frank and Frenchy snatched at their belts for pistols, but before they could bring them level, Frank had three and Frenchy had four arrows buried in their chests. They looked down, then at one another, and they tried to speak, but blood bubbled from their mouths as they fell to their knees and then on their faces, driving the arrows deeper into their chests.

Squirrel started screaming and covered his eyes, but more than half a dozen arrows whispered across the camp to find their places in his chest and neck. He choked on his blood, trying to beg for his life, but no words came. He crumpled to the side, eyes staring at the naked branches of the elm that stretched overhead. For just a brief moment, silence tended the forest, until the war cries and screams of the Osage warriors echoed through the stillness. Ezra stepped forward to be greeted by Eagle's Wing, then both men looked for Gabriel and saw the form of Honey Bear on her knees beside a still form on the forest floor.

31 / Encampment

Three days. Three days of riding, watching, praying. Ezra trailed the two packhorses, while Bear rode her steel dust grey that dragged the travois and led the big black. The pile of buffalo robes kept the still figure warm, but he still lay unconscious and unmoving. His bandages and poultices had stayed the flow of blood, but he had yet to show any sign of life. His breathing was shallow, his movements non-existent, and his color whiter than usual. But Honey Bear stayed by his side all the while, tending his every need.

Dusk had dropped its curtain, and the twilight lay upon the land as the prelude to another time of darkness. But the moon, now full, shed its dim pale-blue light upon the winter encampment of the Osage. When the small band of warriors returned, they received a warm and joyous welcome since they had returned victorious and with all warriors proud of their part in the short battle. Women and children walked beside their men, touching the leggings and looking proudly upon their warrior mates. Blue Corn and Standing Elk watched as the laden travois approached, and the chief looked with concern at Honey Bear. Eagle's Wing stepped down and gave his report of the clash, then pointed at the still form on the travois, "He fought bravely and had killed three of the enemy before he was struck down," explained the war leader. "Bear has tended him and will stay with him."

With no other explanation, Bear led her grey to the bark-covered lodge, and Ezra helped to take Gabriel in and make him comfortable on the pile of buffalo robes. She looked at Ezra and said, "You," nodding to him and Gabe, "will stay in this lodge. Consider it your own. I will tend to his needs, but I will not stay here."

"Whatever you say, Bear," answered Ezra, and with a glance at Gabe, continued, "Do you think he'll come out of it?"

"We must pray and work to do our part, and trust God, or Wah-kon-tah, to do the rest."

She knelt beside Gabe and used a cool damp cloth to wipe his head and face, then began to replace the poultices and bandages.

Ezra brought in their gear, saddles, packs, parfleches, and weapons, then started a small fire for both light and warmth. He tried to stay busy as Bear tended to his friend, but he was worried. It had never been this serious before. Sure, he had been wounded but had proven himself stronger than most and shrugged off the wounds as most would a scratch or bruise. To see his friend unconscious and unmoving and seemingly hanging onto life with no more than a weak grip that appeared to be loosening was hard to handle. He felt helpless, and more than concerned, he was afraid. He was here because Gabe had always been his best friend, more like a brother than just a friend, and they had been inseparable even while Gabe had been in university and he was working with his father. But now he was facing an uncertain future, and he wondered what he would do if his friend did not make it through.

He sucked in a deep breath and sat with his elbows on his knees and his head in his hands, unable to form the words, and allowed the Spirit of God to make intercession for him. God knew his heart, and only God could see them through this time. Memories flitted in and out of his mind, pictures of the two traipsing through the woods as youngsters, hunting together as young men, and laughing together as they dreamed about the time they would become great explorers and adventurers. Other thoughts came of their time together since they left Philadelphia and had fought side by side against river pirates and bounty hunters. Even the times of fighting the Shawnee and the Pawnee brought a smile to his face. Yet now, his thoughts of the future were clouded with concern and even fear. He slowly shook his head and called out to God, "Spare him, Lord. He's a man you can use in so many ways, and he's my friend. Spare him, please."

Bear finished her ministrations, pulled the buffalo robe up and around his shoulders, and sat back on her heels, looking at the still figure. She had tried unsuccessfully to get him to take some broth, succeeding only in getting a little water down his throat, more from a survival instinct than drinking, but it had helped. She looked at Ezra, who sat quietly watching. "He is a strong man. A lesser man would be dead already, but he holds on, and I know he will live."

"But will he be all right? I've known of some men that had a head injury who were never the same afterward," mused Ezra.

"We can only wait," resolved Bear, looking once again at the man who lay so still. Stubble covered his face and his eyes were sunken, but she was determined to see hope where others would have given up and let the patient cross over. "He needs us to fight with him."

He started to reply, but a scratching at the entry turned their attention to the doorway as Grey Fox stepped inside, looked at Ezra with a timid smile, and then at Bear. "I will sit with him while you take time for yourself."

Bear stood and embraced her friend, "I am grateful." Turning to Ezra, she said, "I will return soon. I will stay with him, but I cannot make this lodge my own. You understand?"

"Sure, I understand." He looked at his friend and back at Bear, "We are thankful for all you've done. You are a good friend, Bear."

The fire had chased the chill from the lodge while the smoke filtered its way through the smoke hole, leaving behind a warm glow that comforted all within. Fox had refilled the carved wooden bowl from the water bag fashioned from the stomach of a buffalo and was cooling the forehead of Gabriel with the damp cloth. Ezra watched the tender attention given by this woman he was attracted to, smiling as she worked and showing her concern for this man she barely knew. When she finished, she sat back and looked at Ezra, "You will stay until he is well?"

Ezra smiled, nodding, "Yes, we will stay until he is well."

"It is good. We," she gave a slight nod in his direction, "will come to know one another better." She smiled as she spoke and watched Ezra's reaction to her suggestion.

He smiled back, nodding, "I would like that."

She sat back, still beside the pallet of Gabriel and looked at Ezra, "Tell me about your home and your family."

Ezra smiled and began to share the story of his childhood and youth and of his family. His father the preacher and his mother the black Irish, and the influence of both on his life. He spoke for some time, often prompted by the questions from Fox but willingly sharing his story. It was good to remember and to share, but it also reminded him of his time with Gabriel, this white man who was closer than a brother to him and as much a part of his life as his parents and more. His memories also stirred his curiosity, and after a time, he paused in his recollections. He looked to Fox and said, "Now, you tell me about your life and family."

She leaned back, smiling, and with her hands clasped around one knee, she began. She spoke of her childhood and family. The training she received from her mother and other women in the village, and the guidance given by her father and her uncles. She spoke fondly of her time with the medicine man and his woman, learning of the many herbs and plants that could be used for many purposes. She told of her man, who paid the high price of eight horses to her father for permission to take her as his mate. She had been courted by others but was somewhat surprised that the man who was thought to be one who would become a war leader had chosen her. She spoke fondly of him and told of the births of her children and the battle that had taken her man. It had been a raid against the Kiowa, and although a victorious raid, her man had been wounded and later died. The memory saddened her, but she lifted a smile to Ezra and asked if he had ever had a mate.

"No, no, I haven't."

"But you are a good man and a good hunter. Why have you not taken a woman as your own?" asked Fox, a frown wrinkling her countenance.

Ezra smiled, shook his head gently, and explained, "It is not the same among our people. A man only takes a mate when he wants to spend the rest of his life with one woman and is prepared to make a home for her. Gabe and I had an uncertain future, and it wasn't what you'd call the right time for making a home. But maybe someday."

Their reminiscing was interrupted by the return of Bear, who stepped in and went to the side of Gabriel. She expressed her thanks to Fox and looked to Ezra, "I will stay with him. He will need his bandages changed, and I will try to get him to take some broth. He must take something soon."

Ezra nodded and stood to walk Fox to her lodge. They spoke little as they walked, both enjoying the memories that had been shared, the thoughts that are often treasured but all too regularly are locked away. It was good to think about those things that were the building blocks of their lives, and more so to share them with another. As they neared her lodge, Ezra paused, "It has been good to talk with you, Fox. Thank you for that. I look forward to more times of learning of one another."

She smiled and gently touched his arm, "And I as well, Ezra. Thank you."

When he returned to the lodge, he entered quietly and saw that Bear had made herself a pallet of blankets beside Gabriel and fallen asleep at the side of her patient. He quietly went to his blankets and lay with hands behind his head, staring at the skeleton framework of the lodge and thinking about Fox and their conversation. He glanced at his friend and rolled to his side, facing the wall of the lodge, and drifted off to sleep, thoughts of his future parading through his mind.

32 / Recovery

He smelled smoke and slowly opened his eyes to a dark, blurry image of greys and browns. He blinked to clear the image and began to make out the framework covered with bark. Moving only his eyes from side to side, he saw parfleches stacked against one wall, and an entry that showed dim light around the edges. He turned his head slightly and saw Ezra lying on his side under a heavy buffalo robe, facing him, eyes closed in sleep. He thought that since Ezra was here, they must be with friends. His head pounded with the movement, and he squinted his eyes. His mouth and throat felt dry, and he was powerful hungry. He turned his head the other way and saw Bear lying beside him, hands together under her cheek, and her knees drawn up. He smiled at her nearness and felt good at seeing her.

He tried to swallow but there was no spittle, and he lifted a hand to his throbbing head, felt the bandage, and began to remember. They were in a battle with the bounty hunters, and he felt the blow to his head, then falling into a black void. How long ago was that? The only light in the lodge came from the embers in the fire and the dim light of early morning that tried to squeeze in through the doorway. He breathed deep making a mental check of his body, felt a discomfort in his side, moved his hand there, and found a bandage. There was nothing else that gave any evidence of injury, but he would have to try to stand to know for certain. He pushed away the heavy buffalo robe and pushed up on one elbow but was too weak to do more. He lay back slowly and heard, "*Howa.*"

It was Bear, who rose on one elbow and smiled at him. "How do you feel?"

"How long have I been here, and where is here?" he asked, bewildered.

"You were injured four days ago when we fought the white men."

"Four days? And where are we now?"

"This is the winter encampment of my people. This is where we fought the Pawnee," explained Bear, rising from her blankets and kneeling at his side. She reached out to look closely at the bandage on his head, but he pulled away before sitting still to let her touch his head.

"How bad is that? It is banging inside my head!" He winced as she pulled at the bandage.

"You have lost much blood, and you need to eat. You are healing and will be well soon."

They had spoken in soft voices, but it was enough to bring Ezra awake. He rolled over and sat up, smiling broadly as he looked at Gabe, "Well, 'bout time you woke up. Don't you think a four-day nap is enough?"

"Dunno, gotta wake up first. Can't do that till I get sumpin' to eat!" stated Gabe, grinning, happy to be alive.

It was just a few moments later that Bear sat beside him, holding a cup of warm broth as he struggled to sit up. Once somewhat erect and propped up, he gladly accepted the broth and began to sip at the refreshing liquid. After sating his initial need, he settled back comfortably and looked at Ezra, "So, tell me what happened?"

Ezra chuckled and began, "Well, it all started off all right. You told 'em to whoa up, but the one who went to the woods and was carryin' his rifle thought he'd give it a try, and the two of you traded lead. Then when you let loose on those two near you, I took a shot at the big 'un, but the one 'side him yanked up his pistol and popped one off at'chu. I grabbed a pistol and put one into him, but neither of my shots dropped them fellas, just let out a little blood. But then of a sudden the woods was full of Osage, painted black an' screamin' and layin' lumber into those fellas like they was buildin' a cabin!"

He paused to take a breath and chuckle, "I didn't even have time to get reloaded before it was all over. Eagle's Wing had follered them bounty boys for a couple days but didn't wanna light into 'em till we started the dance. But when they stepped in? Boy howdy, they done a job!"

He looked at Gabe and nodded to Bear, "She's been at your side ever since. Mighty fine medicine she's got, yessir. Course, it helps that you got such a hard head!"

Both Gabe and Bear laughed with Ezra at his remark, but Gabe grabbed at his head, shook it, and said, "Oh, don't do that! That hurts worse'n gettin' kicked by a horse!" He looked at Ezra, "By the way, Ebony all right?"

"Of course. All the horses are fine, especially that big black. But he's been eyein' some o' them mares in that horse herd of the Osage. There might be some black colts come spring!"

A scratch at the door admitted Grey Fox, and she smiled at Ezra and spoke to Gabe, "It is good to see you up!"

"It's mighty good to be up. But, after that broth and all his," nodding to Ezra, "tall tales, I'm already worn out and I think I better lay back down."

Bear agreed, rearranging the hides and blankets for his comfort and helping him to lie down. Once he was prone, she checked his bandages and explained, "I will have to change these before you go back to sleep." Gabe nodded his agreement, watching as she began preparing the poultices by grinding the chosen plants and herbs together to make a paste. She had some bandages already prepared from blanket scraps and strips of cloth and buckskin and worked quickly removing the old ones, cleaning the wounds, and applying the new bandages. She sat back and said, "Now, you rest. I will wake you soon for more broth, and if you do well, maybe something more."

"That 'something more' sounds promising. I'm so hungry my belly button's pinchin' my backbone, so don't spare the 'something more.'"

By the afternoon, he'd had several small feedings and was feeling somewhat better. Although he still had the throbbing in his head, he was optimistic that Bear's ministrations would see him through. She had brewed a tea from the dried blossoms of clematis, periwinkle, and hedge nettle, and assured him it would help with the pounding in his head. He also watched her prepare the poultice, and she explained she used the knapweed and the inner bark of the poplar and some leaves and ground them together to form a pulp for the poultice. She reached into her bag, brought out a small hollowed bone container, and applied a red ointment. "This is also from the poplar. We get this from the buds in the time of greening. The black robes said they called it the 'Balm of Gilead.'"

She was especially attentive to his wounds and said, "I am pleased with the way you are healing. You should be well by the time of greening."

He scowled, "Greening? You mean spring?!" he asked, a little perplexed.

"Yes, it will take time for your head to heal, but more so, for you to heal inside. You will find it difficult to walk straight for some time, but it will come," she explained. "There is no hurry. My people want you to stay the winter with us."

Gabe looked aghast at her, then at Ezra and back, "Stay the winter?"

Ezra chuckled, "Gotta stay somewhere, and this is as good a place as any. Better'n most!"

Gabe put both hands to his head, slowly shaking it side

to side, and reached for the hot tea, "I hope this stuff helps, cuz it tastes like you threw an old moccasin in the water." He slurped a big gulp, struggled to swallow, made a face, and drank some more. Anything was better than thinking about what Ezra had declared about spending the entire winter here in the village. He just wasn't prepared for that.

The scratch at the door gained admittance for Eagle's Wing, who bent down to come into the lodge. He stood, stoic as usual, and looked at both Gabriel and Ezra. When Gabe motioned for him to be seated, the war leader accepted. Once comfortable, he said, "Blue Corn has asked that I speak for our people when I say we would like you to stay with our people through the time of snow. You have been a friend to the Ni-u-kon-ska, and it would be good for you to have a time of healing."

Gabe gazed seriously at Eagle's Wing and answered, "We are honored that you would allow us to be a part of your village, Wing. You and your people have been good friends to us. Ezra tells me I owe you my life. If you and your warriors had not come, I would have crossed over at the hands of those bounty hunters. I am grateful."

"Will you stay, then?" asked Wing.

"It would be good for us to stay, and I believe we could learn from the Osage. We," he nodded at Ezra, "have much to learn about the ways of your people and about the wilderness. Yes, we will stay," resolved Gabe, gaining a smile from both Ezra and Bear.

"It is good," answered Wing, standing to leave. He turned

back and spoke to Gabe, "I will teach you of our people and the way of the wild if you will teach me more of the ways of the white man."

Gabe chuckled, "It will be my privilege!"

Bear's happiness showed in her countenance and work. A broad smile painted her face and remained there throughout the day. She was attentive to the wounds of Gabe and happily prepared his meals, limited though they were, but Gabe enjoyed the broth and was pleased when she added meat to the stew. Fox came often, assisting Bear as needed, but more to visit with Ezra. By evening time, Bear had Gabe standing, although she was doing as much of the standing as he was, holding him with an arm around his waist and his arm around her shoulders. His walking consisted of a walk from the lodge, around the cookfire outside, and back into the lodge. He plopped down on his pallet and leaned forward, hands on his knees, "Whew! That took a lot out of me. This is gonna take longer than I thought," he declared, smiling up at Bear.

"There is no hurry. We will take the time needed, and you will be even stronger than before!" replied Bear, happy with his progress but happier still knowing she was needed by this man.

Gabe looked around the lodge, seeing items hanging from the sides that told of whoever had built and lived in this lodge. He looked at Bear, "Whose lodge is this?"

"Why do you ask?" she replied, looking at Gabe, and around the lodge.

"Well," he started, motioning to the different items that decorated the walls and more, "it's obvious this is someone's home. I don't want to put anybody out."

"This is my lodge," she answered, looking in the satchel that held herbs and plants, and other healing items. "But I will stay with Grey Fox while you are here."

Gabe was speechless, knowing the way they had come to feel about one another, but also knowing of the law of her people that forbad the cohabiting of couples who had not been properly joined by the people. "I see. Would it be better for you if Ezra and I built our own lodge?"

"No. Grey Fox is my friend, and we help one another. It is good for you to stay."

Gabe paused for a moment, looking at this woman who had done so much for him and his friend, "You have done a good thing, taking care of me and more. We are both grateful, but I am more so. Thank you, Honey Bear."

She looked at him with eyes that seemed to see his soul and answered, "We are bound together by Wah-kon-tah. You saved me from the Pawnee and that made me yours. We saved you from the bounty hunters, and that made you mine. We are bound together."

33 / Winter

They walked together, her arm around his waist and his around her shoulders, tentatively taking each step that led them from the lodge. It was his first foray to take him away from the confining quarters, and he breathed deeply of the cool air. He lifted his eyes to the cloud-filled sky, seeing the towering storm clouds with their dark bellies and ever-moving broad shoulders. "Looks like we'll be getting some winter weather soon," he declared, prompting Bear to look to the clouds. "I hope Ezra gets us enough wood. That lodge can get mighty cold when that wind blows."

"But you have many buffalo robes and more to keep you warm," replied Bear, picking her steps along the trail that wound around the camp.

Gabe saw a big log, worn smooth by many sitting on it and polishing the trunk with their movements. He pointed and asked, "How 'bout we sit a spell?"

Bear helped him to be seated, knowing the head injury still

brought spells of dizziness making it hard for him to move quickly. Once situated, he looked around at the naked trees and bushes, some still clinging to their leaves, and asked, "Do your people use this for your winter camp often?"

"We have wintered here before and will again, but our leaders choose our camps and try to avoid using the same ones too often. It gives time for the grasses to replenish and the woods to provide their bounty. When we stay too long, there is not enough firewood or animals for food. And if we return too soon, the Creator has not renewed the woods to provide."

"And the leaders decide when you move?"

"Yes, usually in the time of greening and the time of colors, we move. But there are other times as chosen by the leaders, because of our enemies, or when there are long times without water, or other reasons," she explained.

"And these leaders are Blue Corn, Eagle's Wing, and Standing Elk?" asked Gabe.

"No. We have a council called the Little Old Ones. These are what some would call elders, but they are the keepers of knowledge and have been chosen and gone through the rites to become one. There are men and women on this council, and they are the ones who decide. It is from this council that the chiefs are chosen."

"Are you on this council?" asked Gabe.

"No, but perhaps one day, I shall be chosen. It is a great honor and responsibility to be on the council, and they lead in all things."

The snow began with the usual few flakes drifting slowly to the ground, just enough to tell of more to come. The storm clouds had enveloped the village, and women hurriedly brought in the pots from the outside cookfires and prepared for a long stay in the lodges. As Gabe and Bear hurried back, hobbling as best he could, Ezra and Fox had already brought things in and were readying the noon meal.

It soon became a typical day of the cold season. The four friends spent much time together, and when the women were occupied elsewhere, the men focused their time tending to their weapons, cleaning, repairing, and keeping them always ready for any need. Gabe brought out the few books he had packed for the journey, Blackstone's *Commentaries on the Law*, Voltaire's *Candide*, and the classic tale by Daniel Defoe, *Robinson Crusoe*. While Gabe worked to absorb Blackstone's *Commentaries*, Ezra grabbed *Crusoe* and immersed himself in the grand adventure of a rebellious young man. The women encouraged the men to share the stories in the books, prompting Gabe to turn from Blackstone to Voltaire, for a more entertaining tale.

Once the storm let up, they were surprised to hear a scratch at the door and to see Eagle's Wing enter. "Welcome," said Gabe, seated on his blankets as he watched Fox and Bear tend the cookfire.

Wing seated himself and spoke, "You have been healing well?"

Gabe pointed to Bear, "She says I am, but I think I've got a ways to go. Still havin' a hard time getting around. That wound," touching his hand to the side of his head, "still makes me a little dizzy, but it's getting better."

"Drink!" came the command from a stern-faced Bear, pointing at the cup of Periwinkle tea.

Gabe chuckled, "She says this'll make it better, and it probably has, but I'm about of a mind I'd rather wrestle a mama bear and her cubs than drink this stuff."

Wing grinned and lowered his voice as if to keep the others from hearing, "You do not want to wrestle with Honey Bear, she cheats!"

Everyone laughed, including Honey Bear, who added, "With him, I won't have to cheat. He's too weak, like a rabbit or a squirrel."

"Hey! You just wait till I get better and I'll show you what a squirrel can do when I chase you up a tree!"

Wing looked at Gabe, "When you are stronger, we will go on a hunt. You said you wanted to learn the ways of the wilderness, and I will teach you."

"In the snow?" asked Gabe, a little incredulous.

"Do you not get hungry when there is snow on the ground?" asked Wing somberly.

"Well, yeah, I reckon."

"Then we will go soon," pronounced Wing as he rose to leave.

And they did learn. Eagle's Wing took them on several hunts where they developed their skills at tracking, understanding the behavior of different animals and stalking and moving silently through the woods. Honey Bear and Grey

Fox shared their knowledge of healing plants and herbs and setting snares and traps for small game and about scraping and tanning hides. Blue Corn taught them about flint-knapping and arrow-making.

Gabriel shared his knowledge about the Mongol bow and worked with Eagle's Wing as he sought to build a similar bow, using the way of the Mongols to bend and form the laminated wood. Wing was a patient man and carefully followed Gabe's teaching, but found it difficult to understand the laminating and shaping of the bow. He had crafted many bows in his time and could finish a fine weapon in less than a week, but his envy of the power of the Mongol bow kept him entranced and willing to be patient. In the end, his bow was superior to any he had before, but without the needed materials available, like the ram's horn and the glue from fish bladders, it fell short of the strength of Gabe's bow. He was pleased with his results and was grateful to Gabe, assuring him he would make more and better bows than before.

Ezra had formed a friendship with Standing Elk, and the two had shared with one another about the rifles and pistols of the white man and the use of a war club. Elk was impressed with Ezra's ironwood club and especially the blade from the Spanish halberd. The two worked together to build a similar club for the medicine man.

The friendships developed were strong and mutual. Ezra and Gabe often spent their evenings talking about the people of the village and how much they had learned, not just in skills and habits, but in the way the people depend upon one another and how the entire village was as one family, each caring for the others and seeing that no one went without. Ezra commented, "You know, the way the people have seen to the needs of Grey Fox and her children, that's mighty special. You just don't see that among the so-called civilized folks. Back there, it seems everybody is just out for what they can get or to take care of themselves, and they don't have time for others. It's different with these people, don't you think?"

"I do. But that doesn't mean they're without those who don't quite measure up or don't want to be like the others. But I do like how the people try to keep one another on the right track, and they don't hesitate to send troublemakers on their way. I guess every tribe has those, though. Bear said her brother was one who didn't like the ways of the elders and lit out on his own. She said when one of their own does that, he is dead to them and marked as a renegade," explained Gabe. "Oh, and have you noticed that Crazy Wolf has been hanging around and talking to Grey Fox quite a bit?"

Ezra chuckled, "Yeah, I have. I've talked to him a little, and he seems like a good sort. But I don't know what to think about that. I mean, I like Fox, like her a lot, but I'm not sure what we'll be doin' come spring. It wouldn't be right of me to keep her from what could be a good match if we were to just up and leave. But are we? I mean, are we going to leave come spring?"

Gabe sighed, looking around the lodge that had been their home for the last two months and more, and answered, "I don't know. Bear told me today the elders have asked her to consider being a part of the council. When she talked about it before, she said it was a great honor and one she could not refuse." He twisted around, moving his arms wide back and forth to test the healing of the wound in his side, "I'm pretty well healed up. Haven't been dizzy lately, and the headaches have let up. But . . ."

"Yeah, it's the 'but' that's bothering me too. I really don't see us stayin' and makin' a life with these folks, fine people though they are, but there's too much country to explore and too many things to see and do to settle down. You and me, well, that's just not what I ever thought we'd do, settle down, I mean, or at least not yet."

"I'd have to agree with you," answered Gabe, shaking his head and staring at the fire. "But more than that, even though this all started with the duel and my needing to leave Philadelphia, I believe this is our destiny. Even though we've had plenty of challenges and outlaws chasing us, I think it's more than that. We can't just have our eyes on ourselves and what we think we want to do today or tomorrow. Our country is growing, and we're to grow with it. I truly believe it's our destiny to be the men who explore this country and learn about this great land and share that knowledge with others. Ezra, I think we've discovered our destiny."

Ezra was quiet for a while, staring at the smoldering coals of the fire, then glanced at his friend. "Gabe, you never cease to amaze me. One day you're lying unconscious in the woods, bleeding like a stuck pig and no one knowing if you're gonna see another day, and then here you are, talking about this grand future of exploring the West. I'm sitting here thinking about what we're gonna eat tonight, and you're talking about our destiny." He paused, sighed, and added, "So, I guess it's Westward the Wilderness, eh?"

"Sounds right to me!" answered Gabe, pulling the buffalo robe up around him as he lay back on the pallet of blankets. "Westward the Wilderness!" he whispered.

A LOOK AT: WESTWARD THE WILDER-NESS (STONECROFT SAGA 3)

Osage, Kansa, Otoe, were all tribes west of the Mississippi and dwelt directly in the path of the two friends determined to escape the bounty hunters from Philadelphia and to explore the uncharted wilderness of the west. But when they encounter former French Voyageurs turned slave traders that take Pawnee women captive, their purposes take a turn. But slave-traders are nothing compared to the Omaha and Ponca tribes that have the market cornered on all trade from the Missouri and North Platte Rivers.

But Gabe Stone and Ezra Blackwell, lifetime friends and companions on this journey of discovery, find themselves befriending the Omaha and Ponca and then suddenly paired with the daughter of the most powerful chief in the territory. With every turn they meet a new challenge and just when they think they're on their way into the uncharted wilderness, they are faced with a new challenge. Confronted by a company of Soldado de cuera, the exclusive corps of the Spanish Empire, and a band of Maroons made up of runaway and freed slaves, they have to make a choice that could mean the end of their journey, if not their lives.

AVAILABLE MARCH 2020

ABOUT THE AUTHOR

Born and raised in Colorado into a family of ranchers and cowboys, B.N. Rundell is the youngest of seven sons. Juggling bull riding, skiing, and high school, graduation was a launching pad for a hitch in the Army Paratroopers. After the army, he finished his college education in Springfield, MO, and together with his wife and growing family, entered the ministry as a Baptist preacher.

Together, B.N. and Dawn raised four girls that are now married and have made them proud grandparents. With many years as a successful pastor and educator, he retired from the ministry and followed in the footsteps of his entrepreneurial father and started a successful insurance agency, which is now in the hands of his trusted nephew. He has also been a successful audiobook narrator and has recorded many books for several award-winning authors. Now finally realizing his life-long dream, B.N. has turned his efforts to writing a variety of books, from children's picture books and young adult adventure books, to the historical fiction and western genres.

ℓ

Printed in Great Britain
by Amazon